Sign up for book announcements and special deals at:

AWBALDWIN.COM

Highly recommended!"

--Landon Beach, Amazon Bestselling Author and
Grand Master Adventure Writers Award Finalist

"A hoot of an adventure novel…"

--Readers' Favorite Five Star Review

RAPTOR CANYON

A moonshining hermit
A big-city lawyer
A $35million con job

A gin-brewing recluse, Relic watches from afar as three men reveal a panel of petroglyphs that include the yawning jaws of a flesh-eating dinosaur. When one of the men murders the other, Relic is on the march to uncover what's going on in Raptor Canyon.

As a fresh graduate, Wyatt is anxious to make his mark among the army of lawyers in a respected Denver law firm. When his boss invites him to tour a client's development project bordering Canyonlands National Park, Wyatt jumps at the chance, but his boss is not what he seems…

When a treacherous security chief tries to kill Relic, Wyatt is caught in the deadly chase. An unusual pair, Wyatt and Relic must tolerate each other while fleeing through white-water rapids, remote gorges, and hidden caverns. Relic devises a plan to save the treasured canyon but Wyatt must come to terms with the cost to his career if he fights his powerful boss…

A college student with secret ties to the site, Faye joins the kitchen crew so she can spy on the enigmatic project. She catches Relic and Wyatt red-handed, preparing for action. But when she hears their desperate plan, she has a decision to make...

Armed with a full box of toothpicks (and a *little* dynamite), can the unlikely trio monkey-wrench the corrupt land deal and recast the fate of Raptor Canyon?

****

WINGS OVER GHOST CREEK

A moonshining hermit.
A reluctant pilot.
A $5million plunder.

Owen discovers a murdered corpse at a college-run archaeological dig in the Utah outback but when he and a park service pilot try to reach the sheriff for help, their plane is shot from the sky. Owen must ditch the aircraft in the Colorado River, where he is saved by a gin-brewing recluse named Relic. The offbeat pair flee from the sniper and circle back to warn the students but not everyone there is who they seem... The two must trek through rugged canyon country, unravel a baffling mystery, and foil a remarkable form of thievery. Suzy, a student at the dig, helps spearhead their escape but the unique team of crooks has a surprise for them…

Can they uncover the truth and escape an archeology field class that hides assassins and dealers in black-market treasure?

"*Wings Over Ghost Creek* is a beautifully written thriller."
-*Readers' Favorite* Five Star Review

"Baldwin delivers another gripping Relic tale with trademark wit and deft expression. This is adventure with philosophy that keeps you nodding your head long after you've put the book down."
– Jacob P. Avila, *Cave Diver*, Grand Master Adventure Writers Award Winner

"*Wings Over Ghost Creek* is a humorous, fun, and well-plotted adventure. Baldwin is a master storyteller, and you will enjoy spending some time with his main character, Relic."
-Landon Beach, Bestselling Author of *The Sail*

Readers' Favorite says:

Wings provides "funny, zippy dialogue"

"[The] plot is lively and exciting"

"suspense and action…keep[s] readers turning the pages until the very end"

Relic brings "another level of wit and humor to the piece throughout"

"A quirky mix of adventure, mystery and the great outdoors"

"characters are credible and finely honed"

"sure to be a hit with lovers of ancient history and crime thrillers alike"

"totally mad chase scenes"

"most highly recommended"

Five Star Review from Readers' Favorite

DESERT GUARDIAN

A moonshining hermit.
A campus bookworm.
A midnight murder.

Ethan's world turns upside-down when he slips off the edge of red-rock cliffs into a world of twisting ravines and coveted artifacts. Saved by a mysterious desert recluse named Relic, Ethan must join a whitewater rafting group and make his way back to civilization. But someone in the gorge is killing to protect their illegal dig for ancient treasures... When Anya, the lead whitewater guide, is attacked, he must divert the killer into the dark canyon night, but his most deadly pursuer is not who he thinks... Ethan struggles to save his new friends, face his own mortality, and unravel the chilling murders. But when they flee the secluded canyon, a lethal hunter is hot on their trail...

Can an unlikely duo and a whitewater crew save themselves and an ancient Aztec battlefield from deadly looters?

Reviews on Amazon say:

"full of suspense…you will be deeply involved from the moment you begin."

"ingenious plot, gorgeous setting, intriguing characters, great read."

"loved the mysterious character *Relic*."

Readers' Favorite says:

Desert Guardian is an "engaging action… mystery."

The novel features "tough, credible characters"

"A.W. Baldwin's writing is clear, fluid, and very detailed."

"… a book that's well worth reading"

Five Star Review from Readers' Favorite

A.W. BALDWIN

WINGS OVER GHOST CREEK

ISBN   978-0-9996913-8-0 Hardbound
ISBN   978-0-9996913-9-7 Paperback
ISBN   978-0-9996913-7-3 ebook

Cover art by Daniel Thiede.
Map art by Nathan Baldwin.

In Memory of
Norman Willow

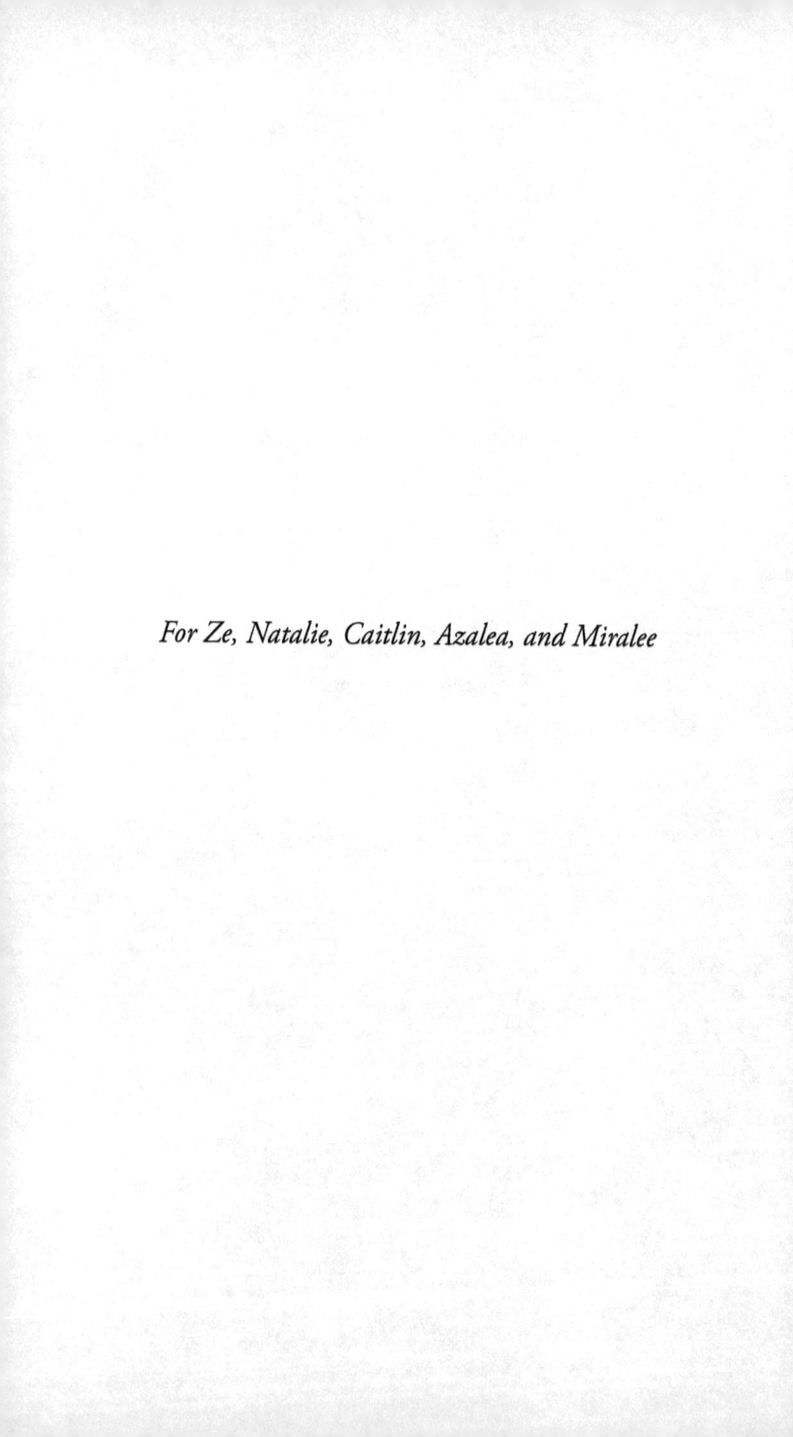

For Ze, Natalie, Caitlin, Azalea, and Miralee

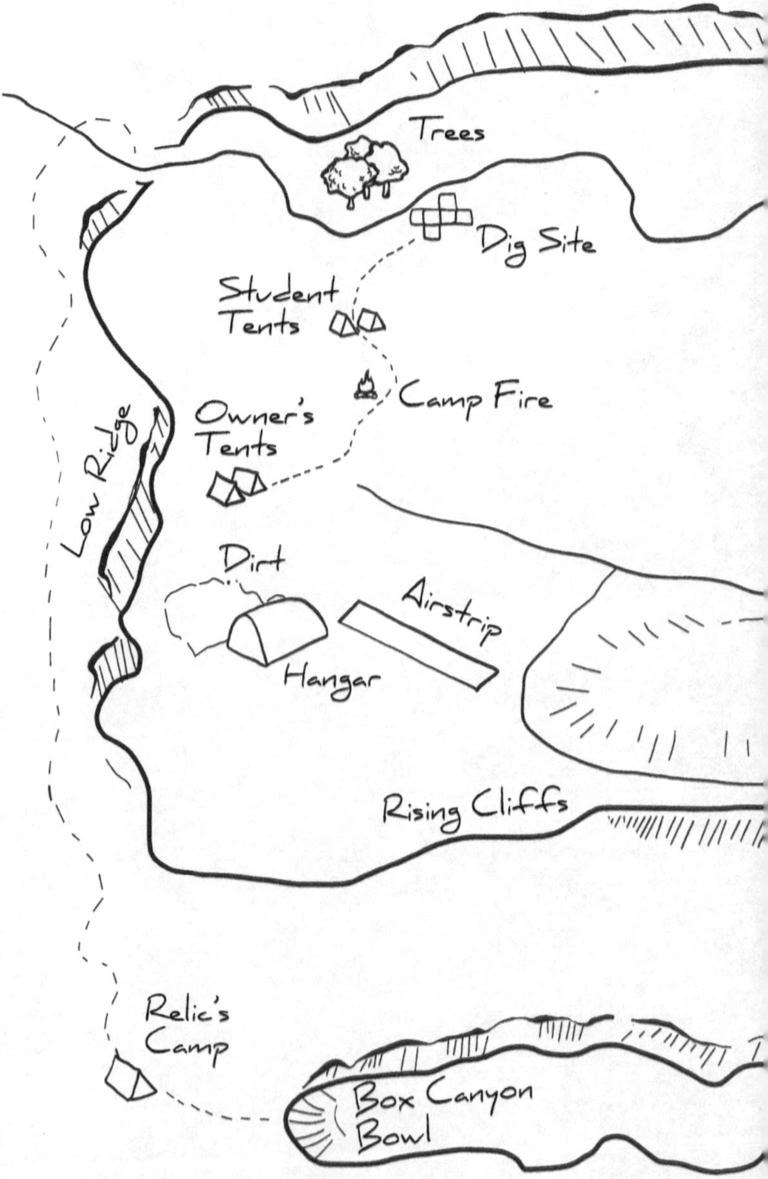

Trees
Dig Site
Student Tents
Camp Fire
Low Ridge
Owner's Tents
Dirt
Airstrip
Hangar
Rising Cliffs
Relic's Camp
Box Canyon Bowl

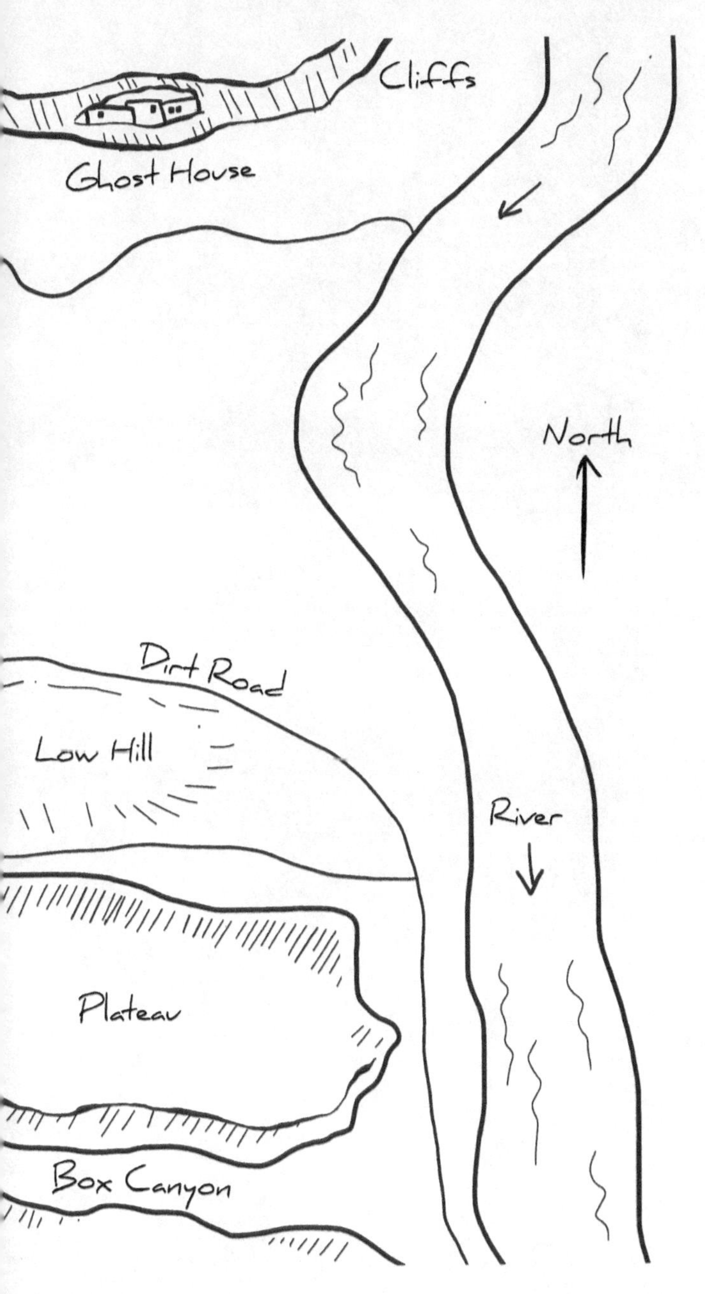

Cliffs
Ghost House
North
Dirt Road
Low Hill
River
Plateau
Box Canyon

CHAPTER 1

"I don't know whether to scratch my head... or my butt."

Relic belly-crawled away from the sandstone ledge and set his binoculars at his feet. He pulled calloused fingers through his hair and combed it into a tight ponytail. A black goatee dangled from his chin, its wiry threads stirring in the breeze. A part-time moonshiner and full-time wanderer, Relic traced much of his genetic soup to the Hopi and Scottish tribes, one-quarter cup each, a recipe for autonomy. He moved to the edge of the cliff again and gazed across the plateaus. Ashen clouds piled atop each other and were sliding across the western mesa.

For two days now, he'd been watching the camps below from a set of pristine ruins tucked into the auburn cliffs. An organized archeological dig was underway two hundred feet below him, across a perennial creek that meandered below the ancestral Hopi townhouses. Twelve small hiking tents formed a semi-circle around a fire pit and the nearby dig. To the right, a makeshift kitchen completed the camp. Each afternoon, a woman with a single, blonde braid led discussions under a canopy near the propane stove.

Another hundred yards away, three family-style tents rested at the base of a long ridge of loose rock. To the side, a pile of dirt nearly six feet high angled away from the natural formation. Two large tarps were hung from a weather-worn Quonset hut and hid a stretch of the ridge and dirt from view. Three men slept in those big tents, separate from the diggers, though they interacted with them from time to time. A man with round glasses had driven away this morning, maybe on some kind of errand. The archeological activity seemed pretty straightforward, but those tarps to the side were hiding something...

Relic raised the binoculars to his eyes.

Someone in a red cap stood behind the Quonset hut, a bolt-action rifle slung across his bony shoulder. He was turning something life-sized. Was he dancing with someone? Tying something up? Relic focused more carefully.

"I'll be damned…"

That thing the man was fiddling with wore a checkered shirt as stiff as a board, a weird, round face with grimaced lips and triangle eyes, like the ones painted on Halloween pumpkins.

There haven't been fields of corn in this dried up, crop-less desert, Relic thought, since the ancient ones abandoned it a thousand years ago. Yet the skinny man with the rifle carried a full-sized, bona fide scarecrow, a bright red circle painted on the center of its chest.

CHAPTER 2

Everett pulled a tarnished handle on the screen door, its aluminum latch missing. Round, wire-rimmed spectacles gave him a certain home-boy look, open and polite. He slipped on his best smile and poked his head inside.

"Hello? Is anyone home?"

Blue-gray curtains blocked the probing sun, casting the room in ashen tones. Family portraits hung on paneled walls by the window. The air was stale and warm, a metal box fan sitting listlessly in the corner.

Everett tugged at his yellow tie, already feeling some early summer heat exhaling from the lunch-box trailer. He put one foot on the landing.

"Hello?" He leaned past the threshold.

Someone lay sprawled in a leather recliner, mouth lopsided and open, long, white hair spread over her shoulders.

"Hello?"

The woman did not move.

He stepped into the trailer, let the aluminum door bang shut, and watched her closely. She didn't wince, blink, or shift in her chair. He rocked slowly on his heels as he glanced around the room.

A kitchenette opened to his right, white propane stove in the middle, enamel chipped along the edges. Formica, its wood-block laminate tired and worn, extended along the kitchen wall and turned ninety degrees to form a partial boundary for the living room. Catalogs, letters, and papers stacked and spread across the top, a copy of last month's "House Beautiful" peeking through the pile.

He glanced at the elderly woman again and stepped closer to the documents. Gingerly, he moved the scattered papers aside, examining them for anything of interest. There, a few pages down, was a bill of sale of some sort, for a vehicle, with her name and scribble at the bottom.

Everett removed his cell phone from its holster. Centering the paper, he snapped a quick picture, returned the phone to its usual setting, and put it away.

He looked at the woman again, her head still jack-knifed backwards, her narrow lips open, her gaunt form casting a spell across the room. He needed to break the spectral silence, chase the eeriness away. He cleared his throat.

"Are you all right?" The sound of his own words reassured him a bit, and he stepped closer to her. "Hey, are you all right?" His voice became more urgent.

Everett moved next to the woman and stared down at her. Her hands, open and frail, lay motionless across her lap. Her chest did not seem to rise or fall with breath and her face appeared cadaverous in the shuttered light.

Everett peered at her hands as he had at his own grandmother's when he was only a boy, staring as if he could wake her from a dream and find that life was still within her, even in the open casket. The memory, risen from the deep so quickly, unnerved him.

He moved even closer to the old woman and whispered to himself, "Oh, my god, she's..."

Her coal-brown eyes suddenly blinked open.

"Crap!" He threw his arms back, stepped away, and sucked a deep breath of air.

She stared at him.

"Oh, god, I thought you were...I thought..." He exhaled slowly and touched his chest. "I didn't know if..." he shook his head and glanced at the floor, "...if you were...all right."

"What are you doing in my house?" she asked, straightening her dress, the vision of his grandmother coming back to life. He sat quickly onto the couch, brushing at the upholstery and the memory of his first funeral.

"Do you mind if I sit? No, no, you don't mind, do you?" He heard his voice raise an octave and he took another deep breath, trying to remember what he'd come here to say. He straightened his tie and tried to collect his thoughts.

"I work for Wyndotte College. I'm here to talk to you about leasing a couple of acres next semester, out by Ghost Creek, for a dig, for our archeology students. Where the old airstrip is."

"I didn't ask you to come into my house." She sat up in the recliner, pushing the footrest to the floor. She rose slowly, using her arms to brace herself, the leather chair creaking.

"I know. I'm sorry. I knocked and no one answered so I peeked in." He waved his hand toward the door.

She pulled her walker from behind the chair and unfolded it, a metal envelope on hinges. "What do you want, again? I don't want any more subscriptions..."

"No, no. I'm not selling anything." He pushed his glasses tighter against his face and tried another smile. "The college wants to lease a small piece of your land to let our archeology students participate in a dig. It's a small piece, but thanks to a donation, we can offer you a nice bonus for signing." He rolled his head, trying to relax the muscles in his neck.

"I don't want your bonus," she stepped forward, her hands on the walker. "I don't want your sweepstakes or your lease."

"No, no sweepstakes, ma'am. Just a lease. I thought surely you'd consider it, I mean, for the students." He rubbed his hand across his forehead. "And the bonus would bring you some serious money."

She shuffled closer to him. "You need to go now."

"But…" he stood up from the couch and stepped back.

She slid her walker toward him and moved to the center of it.

"The bonus this year is more than generous, and besides…"

She lifted her walker in the air with surprising agility and poked its rubber-bottomed legs at him. He stepped away too quickly, his left foot jammed against his right, his center of gravity unhinged and he toppled backwards, his arms reaching for empty air, his torso twisting down onto the carpet with a thud.

Damn it, he'd bit his tongue. Loops of dirty carpet, enlarged by their proximity, filled his field of vision. He tried to refocus. "Just let me explain..." He looked up at her.

Her mouth clamped shut, her dark eyes narrowed, and she marched closer to Everett, her walker jabbing feebly in the air.

"Please..." He retreated politely, scooting along the floor.

She moved steadily toward him.

"Oh, come on now, this is ridiculous," he cried, crawling on hands and feet along the carpet, reaching for the door and pushing it open. "Gawdammit," he protested and rolled outside to safety.

Shit.

But he had what he needed anyway.

CHAPTER 3

They searched each other's eyes, the intensity of the moment crackling between them. Her heart-shaped face was a little crooked, angling her grin to the left, and he loved it. Her eyes gleamed like tiny spotlights behind stained-glass windows, not quite blue, not quite hazel, and could cast a wicked glare when she wanted.

Tonight they were grabbing their future with all four hands and escaping this tiny, dead-end town forever.

"It's time." Liz turned and tossed the empty duffle bags into the '84 Toyota pickup and slid into the passenger seat.

Though she was one year older than he, they were both seniors in high school, misfits who fit together in dogged determination to leave their lives of poverty and isolation and forge careers for themselves in Los

Angeles, complete with new names and identities and lifestyles. They'd imagined and planned and disputed it all with hurried whispers and stolen kisses in the back of the cafeteria and the sun-bleached seats of his brother's pickup.

Full of dread and excitement, Robbie stomped his cowboy boots in the dirt and rounded the truck.

They'd waited until 10:00 p.m. sharp, when they knew the small town museum that Liz cleaned on Saturdays would be dark and empty. She had the back door alarm code to the Upper Valley Historical Center and an extra key, and she knew where valuable artifacts were kept in the back, accessible without threat of the forward alarms that were wired to the public displays.

He cranked the engine, pumping fuel into the old carburetor until it coughed to life.

He glanced at Liz, who kept her eyes forward, relaxed but intent on the road before them. He turned the wheel and drove slowly from her grandmother's house, where Liz had a small bedroom in the attic. They drove along Second Street for nearly a mile. He glanced again and she looked as cool as the slushies they'd drink in the evenings – lime with a shot of her grandma's tequila in them. A poor man's margarita, Liz had called it. Totally gross. But not bad enough to toss down the drain either.

He turned right one block short of Main Street and scanned the empty road ahead.

Suddenly, white-hot flashes strobed across the rearview mirror and Robbie nearly emptied his bladder. Speechless, he swerved a bit before coasting to the curb.

"Shit." He set the brake.

"It's OK. We're just cruising around. He'll just tell us to go home." Liz reached across the seat and squeezed Robbie's hand, and the warmth of it let him breathe again. He nodded and watched in the side mirror as the deputy stepped out of his car, adjusted his belt, and strode to the truck.

Robbie rolled down the window. A flashlight glared into his eyes and he closed them for a moment.

"Robert?" The deputy shined his light across Robbie's lap and onto Liz.

"Yeah. What's up, deputy?" His words sounded stupid as soon as he said them and he squeezed Liz's hand a little tighter.

"Out kinda late on a Sunday, aren't you?" Blue and white strobes made the officer's face flash cold and hot, his eyes hollow, his lips wooden.

Robbie shivered.

"What's your story tonight?"

Robbie took a breath. "Just cruising, officer."

They both knew Deputy Robinson. He'd busted them for smoking pot behind the football field last fall, and they'd been released to a so-called juvenile rehabilitation program that only left them more frustrated than ever. But Robbie knew that tonight he'd have to stay polite and obedient. Until they could make their move.

"Right…"

"Nothin' wrong with that, is there?" Robbie heard the annoyance in his voice and tried to throttle it back. He released Liz's hand and rested it on the steering wheel. "I mean, we're just driving around." He looked toward Liz and back at Robinson.

"You haven't been drinking tonight, have you?"

"No, sir. See…" he exhaled toward the officer. "Clean breath."

Robinson leaned away from the window. "Sure."

Robbie opened the palms of his hands in a gesture of innocence. The deputy flashed his lantern across them again and turned it off.

"Just checking in with you, Robert. Keep it clean and we'll have no troubles. Finish your drive and get this young lady back home, by," he looked at his watch, "10:40. OK?"

"Yes, sir."

"I'll stop you again if I see you after that, right?"

"Yes, sir." Robbie rolled up his window and glanced nervously at Liz. He turned on the radio but kept the sound low, a soft country tune soothing the adrenalin back out of his system.

He released the brake, slid the shifter into first, and moved cautiously along the street, watching his rearview mirror.

Deputy Robinson turned off his strobe lights, made a tight U-turn, and drove away.

"You did great, Robbie." Liz slid closer to him and put her hand on his thigh. He took a deep breath and smiled, the warmth of her touch flooding him with a sense of courage.

"Yeah, well, when we're done tonight, that asshole will never bother us again."

"Damn right."

He turned onto Charles Street, watching the road behind to make sure there was still no sign of Deputy Robinson. Halfway down the block, he turned into the lot behind the museum, turned the truck around, and backed close to the rear door. He shut off the engine, its final knock fading into silence.

They sat there for several moments, letting the quiet and the weight of their next steps settle in.

"Ready?" His voice croaked.

She looked at him expectantly and grabbed the duffle. "Let's go."

Robbie reached to the ceiling and turned off the overhead light. They hopped out of the truck in the dark, and Liz went quickly to the rear entrance and opened the door. Inside, she entered the security code and a little red light blinked out.

"Come on," she waved at Robbie.

He looked around outside, then scooted past the threshold and closed the door behind him.

Liz turned on a small flashlight and went quickly past the restrooms and entered a doorway to their right. Robbie flicked on his light and followed her.

CHAPTER 4

Inside, they swept their lights across the room. A row of narrow tables lined the wall to their right, miscellaneous items scattered across them. Rows of shelves and drawers stretched before them like book stacks in a library. He could see Liz counting each row as she walked along, stopping at the sixth one. He hurried to the same row and walked behind her.

Wide cabinets stretched before them, individual drawers half the height of ordinary dresser drawers and, instead of knobs to pull, two hand-sized openings were carved into the top of each. He stopped at the nearest one and gently slid it open.

Rows of mismatched, U-shaped objects filled the space, their shadows harsh and unsteady under his roving light. He picked one up. The size and shape of a horseshoe, the thing yawned at the ends into flattened pieces with subtle ball joints. A coded number appeared on the side in black ink. Dark bore holes lined the narrow rim, jagged and empty.

"Shit, Liz, this is somebody's jaw!"

"Shhh…"

He quickly put the toothless bone back in its place. "There's nothing but jaws in this drawer," he whispered. "People's jaw bones, and no skulls…"

"Shhh…"

"Why would they have a drawer full of jaws?" He searched up and down the aisle, as if the rest of the skeletons would be lurking nearby.

"Three, four, five," Liz whispered, pointing her finger at a bank of the shallow drawers marked with numbers like the Dewey decimal system. She opened the fifth drawer and they peered inside.

Rows of chert arrowheads and knife blades filled the front of the drawer. Liz reached behind the flint-like tools, deep into the back of the drawer, and pulled a soft, folded cloth to the front.

"Put your light on it." She unwrapped the white cotton carefully, exposing four clay figurines tucked into sewn-in pockets. She pulled the first one out.

Robbie's heart beat faster and his face flushed.

The figurine was about one-and-a-half inches wide and five inches tall. A round, pale head was formed and decorated with small notches above a pair of line-drawn eyes. Tiny holes encircled its neck and chips of sea shell wound its waist like a belt. Lines showed where the arms lay, and what seemed like a kilt was sketched across its thighs. More markings decorated its feet.

"This one is a man." She slid it back into its cotton sleeve. "Clarence, the curator, says these came from an old Hopi family up on the mesas, back in the 1920s. But they're a thousand years old, he said, worth maybe thirty-five thousand dollars apiece."

Robbie released a slow whistle.

"They say the nicer ones are on display, but these are more interesting and worth almost as much." She folded the cloth over the figures and reached into the duffle.

"Are these enough?" Robbie shifted his light to the knives and arrowheads. "Should we take some of these, too?"

"Yes, we should take them, too, but they have to be wrapped almost as carefully or they'll chip." She removed a terrycloth towel and wrapped the figurines in it, enlarging the bundle to the size of a giant dictionary. "Here, take one of the other towels and roll up the bigger pieces."

He laid the towel on the floor and placed a knife on one corner, rolled it partway up, placed another knife on the towel and repeated the process until it was full.

Liz took another towel, moved several rows down and pulled out another drawer. Robbie tucked the stone artifacts into the duffle and shined his light on Liz. She lifted several decorative clay plates, wrapped them in soft cloth and newspaper, and duct-taped them closed.

The clunking sound of metal on metal shattered their concentration and they stared at each other for a terrified moment.

"The front door! Someone's trying to get in the front door!" Liz zipped the duffle closed and turned off her flashlight.

Robbie turned back to see the way they'd come in, swinging his light with him, then clicked it off. "What the hell?" he whispered.

"Sounded like the front door."

"Who would try to open that at this hour?"

"I don't want to find out."

"Let's get the hell out of here." He heard Liz close the drawers of artifacts. He felt her touch, then push him forward in the dark. It propelled him with a rush of electricity down his spine, into his legs. He sprinted down the narrow space between the stacks, slid around the corner and across the open linoleum floor, slamming into the exit door, heaving for oxygen.

"Slow down." Liz came close up against him and opened the door carefully. They both took a step into the outer hallway.

A spotlight reached into the museum through the plate glass window on Main Street, feeling its way along the walls, flashing across the public exhibits, tossing shadows like grim reapers searching for their victims. Robbie held Liz's arm and tried to breathe.

"Now," Liz led them back along the hall toward the exit, deeper into the dark, farther from the harsh light and swirling shadows.

She opened the back door and peered outside. "Come on."

They ran to the truck, opened the doors and slid into the seat. Liz placed the duffle bags at her feet and clipped on her seatbelt. Robbie turned the key and quickly put the truck into first gear.

She reached across the seat and put her hand on his arm. "Slow, no lights."

He eased across the lot, gravel popping under the tires like fireworks. The truck lurched over the curb and onto Charles Street again and he turned left, away from the front of the museum. He shifted into second gear and navigated by memory along the dark street.

"Turn right up here." Liz craned her neck, watching behind them as they went.

As Robbie turned the wheel, they both saw a pair of headlights swing into the back lot of the museum, then swing back out just as fast, police lights now spinning their disorienting alarm, turning toward them, spotlight leading the way.

Robbie finished his turn and hit the gas pedal hard, flying though third gear and rushing away from town in the pitch black of night. They saw the deputy's car moving at a deliberate pace, searching with its lights, not yet in pursuit.

They raced along the back road, rising over small bumps, smashing back down on worn-out shocks, hoping to hell they wouldn't crash into a bike or a skateboard ramp or some other junk left haphazardly on the residential street. The police lights seemed to be following them, but Robbie could not be sure. He disengaged the clutch.

"No brake lights!" Liz yelled. "Don't brake!"

He downshifted into first and the engine whined in protest as Robbie turned right, out of the deputy's line of sight, along another block, then into second gear on Main Street and straight out of town on the state highway, into third gear, then fourth, before he dared to turn his headlights back on.

"Holy flying shit," Robbie pounded the dashboard and looked to Liz.

"Holy Bonnie and Clyde!" She reached across and kissed him hard on the lips and he nearly lost control.

CHAPTER 5

Adrenalin drove Robbie and Liz deep into the night without food or rest or loss of focus. By midnight, they'd finally reached a dirt road turnout along the state highway, their first destination. Robbie pulled in and slid the pickup out of gear.

They looked at each other again, almost too nervous to speak.

"This is where we turn off," Robbie reached his hand for hers.

"You trust this Johnson guy to meet us?"

"I'm telling you, I knew him from school."

"He's way older than us," Liz said.

"He graduated with my brother Ed."

"OK." She took a breath and squeezed his fingers. "I know all this. I'm just nervous."

"You?" he tried to chuckle.

"Me," she poked at his ribs and showed him that crooked smile.

"We're almost there. We take this dirt road to a spot behind the hill. That's where Johnson will meet us, then we'll all go to his place, out of the way, where it's safe. We'll do our deal there. We wait 'till nightfall again, then hit the road to Cedar City…"

"Ed will get the truck there?"

"Yep. We'll leave it by the bus station. Then we take the bus to L.A. New names. Clean start," he nodded.

"L.A." Her hazel-blue eyes stared through the window and into the distance.

"The first thing we do, I'm buying you a real margarita."

"You know the way to my heart." She batted her eyelashes.

"We've got pads and sleeping bags in the back of the truck."

"That's not all you've got on your mind, is it?" She looked at him sideways, mischief in her voice. "Sleeping, I mean…"

He looked away sheepishly. "Let's get off the highway." He put the truck into first gear and turned down the dirt road, riding over the washboard surface as fast as he dared. Two miles away, the road degraded to a two-track path and turned behind a large hill that hid them from the road and all of civilization. Nervously, he stopped at a level spot and turned off the lights and ignition. She reached for his hand and pulled him across the seat and out the door with her. They scrambled into the bed of the truck and forgot about everyone and everything else in the universe, long into the early morning hours.

CHAPTER 6

Owen scrolled down his phone, checking Facebook posts, stopping to read featured messages, like the one about how not to wash a kangaroo. The room hummed with low sounds of movement, people shifting in their chairs, sliding papers, whispered messages. He glanced up.

A deputy county sheriff began writing on the large white-board, his beige uniform stretched tightly across his back. "Here are the museums that have been robbed to date…"

Owen stared at the icons on his phone. Six years ago, his father died of leukemia. Devastated, Owen and his mother moved in with Owen's uncle, who barely tolerated them. Two months later, Owen was arrested for pulling a stupid stunt with a high school pal who thought it would be a thrill to rob the local gas station store. Owen was the "getaway" driver, but they'd been caught immediately, before they even left the parking lot. His pal had one of those realistic cap guns, and he'd colored over the orange ring on the end of the barrel, the one to let people know it was a fake. "Easy peasy, cash is squeezy," his pal had said, over and over, smiling at the stupid phrase. He'd never seen the guy again and never wanted to.

Owen was sentenced as a juvenile and assigned to a sixty-three-year-old probation officer folks called Probation Officer Pete. Owen's mother pushed him to test for college entrance exams, and he finally did, scoring in the eighty percentile range. But Pete pushed him toward law enforcement instead, having him visit with detectives, beat cops, highway patrol officers, learning what they did and why they did it. He admired law enforcement but, really, Pete was the one who should have been the cop. Owen once asked about a training program for young pilots, but Pete told him flight school wasn't realistic, that Owen should focus on staying anchored, figuratively and literally. Now, Owen was nearly three years past probation and his juvenile record was closed and sealed. But once or twice a month, he still talked with Pete, who ended his calls with the rote advice: "Stay grounded, stay safe."

Last spring, Pete helped Owen get a job with the National Park Service in Williamsburg, handing out maps at the entry gates, directing lost tourists to restrooms. Then cutbacks and management changes landed Owen a six-month gig in the Utah back-country. No jostling crowds here. No reconstructed law offices, no blacksmiths, historical re-enactments, carriages, white wigs, lace-up shoes, or cute summer interns. He hated it.

The deputy turned back to the group and Owen straightened in his chair. The meeting was a briefing of federal park rangers, state investigators, and some of their support staff. Even an FBI agent was said to be in attendance.

"So far, we think each of these robberies was carried out by separate perpetrators, for a couple of reasons. For one, the level of sophistication varies. In one case, robbers disabled a pretty complicated alarm system. In other cases, it was just a 'smash and grab.' And the locations around the state, and the timing, also make us think each robbery was carried out by separate thieves. But what's intriguing is that they all went for the back-room, valuable artifacts. Nothing from the public display cases, where immediate alarms would have had us scrambling. So they had a common theme, maybe a common influence or strategy. They focused on Pueblo I, II, and III artifacts – all eras of ceramics, tools, footwear, clay figurines, even a turkey feather blanket, were stolen."

"Feather blanket?" someone asked.

"Sure. They raised turkeys and it gets cold in the winter," he shrugged. "Don't forget, these cultures were pretty advanced, with urban centers at Chaco Canyon, among other places, and trading routes all through the four corners region, on down into Mexico."

A woman behind Owen spoke up. "As with Rome, all roads lead to Chaco Canyon..."

"And information helping us capture these guys leads to a fifty thousand dollar reward."

Mumbles rose from the group.

The deputy nodded. "So, back to our theory. If we're right, some deep thought has gone into a coordinated effort here, and it's likely to have come from traffickers."

Owen's eyes widened. He'd had no idea.

A heavyset man in the back raised his hand and asked: "Any leads on that end?"

"Harvey, want to fill us in?" the deputy looked at a thin man in a white shirt and blue tie in the front row.

"Our field office in Florida, near Sarasota, has

some unverified intel that a known trafficker has been especially active lately, with meetings, phone calls, trips to the bank. We don't have enough for a warrant, but it sure feels like his busy season all of a sudden. We're working the money end of it, trying to see if we can figure out how he may be financing his purchases, presumably of stolen artifacts. We'll keep the sheriff updated as we can."

The deputy nodded. "And one of our thieves was caught on video, black and white, for just a moment. No view of his face, unfortunately. Male, six feet tall, medium build, Hawaiian-style shirt, dark hair in a ponytail."

"Hey," the heavyset man in back raised his hand again. "Does that remind us of our mystery man?"

"A little."

"Who?" the FBI agent turned to ask.

"Just a rumor…" the deputy replied.

"More than just," the heavy man shook his head. "We've had reports of a moonshiner way back in the canyons, same general description. There's a ten thousand dollar reward for finding him. Average height, black ponytail, trespassing on federal lands, property destruction, unlicensed alcohol manufacture…"

"They barely qualify as reports…" the deputy

shook his head.

"More like sightings," said the woman behind Owen.

"Let's keep our eye out for Bigfoot, folks," someone said, and they all relaxed with a chuckle.

CHAPTER 7

"All right, everyone, let's all pull up a camp chair and take a seat."

Suzy watched as Angela Lazarus glanced at her notes on the folding table and waited for the students to sit. She looked like she was in her mid-forties, fit, loose long-sleeve shirt open over a T-shirt, broad-rimmed gardener's hat on her head. Blonde hair hung in a single braid down her neck. She could be a student…

The field course was offered for two-and-a-half week periods over the spring and summer months. Introduction to Archeologic Excavation was taught by Professor Combs, a man considered brilliant in his younger days, but, according to campus gossip, now deep in the seductive grip of alcohol or opioids, or both, leaving his aide more and more frequently to plan and present his classes, grade his students' papers, and sign his name for the registrar. There was a rumor that he would not actually participate in the course.

"Thank you. What a beautiful morning to resume our seminar and what a great location." Angela pointed to Ghost House Ruins some eight hundred yards away and two hundred feet above them. She spoke with relaxed authority, and the students listened in earnest.

"Just a couple of quick items to cover this morning. To begin, please stop calling me Ms. Lazarus or professor, or such. I am Professor Comb's aide, Angela," she touched her chest, "and we should be on a first name basis by now."

Several students nodded.

"One student already asked, so I'll let everyone know. Those of you expecting Professor Comb to arrive later in the schedule will not, I hope, be too disappointed. The professor has been ill and is no longer expected to join us for this course."

Rumor confirmed, Suzy thought.

"Not to worry, though, as I have been certified as an adjunct professor for this class and, most importantly," she raised a finger, "it still gets you all of the required 'lab' credits for your science requirements, in only sixteen days…"

This elicited some embarrassed nods and chuckles.

"Again, if you've brought your personal items in

a daypack, as instructed, you've got all you need. Tents, bags, pads, food, and transportation have been provided – that's what those lab fees are for."

She pointed to the cliffs on the other side of the creek. "Known as the Spirit or Ghost House Ruins, those homes were built some 1600 years ago by masons of the Fremont people, ancestral families of the modern day Pueblo. Though those ruins are beautiful and tempting, I want to say again that we will not excavate anywhere close to them. They are on federal property and we have no permission to dig there. We can take a tour up to the site sometime, but no one is to touch or enter those ruins, which are protected. Our location, here," she pointed to the ground, "is on private land under a lease to the college from the landowner. We are only permitted to conduct our dig about fifty feet from the current creek bed. But do not be dismayed," she smiled. "Creeks like this meander over time and Pueblo settlements often included temporary shelters by the water, where communities would butcher game or turkeys, engage in races or contests of skill, or just plain socialize. We think this is an excellent site to explore."

A student to Suzy's left raised his hand. "We stopped work on the site around three o'clock yesterday. Will that be the usual schedule?"

"Because of the potential for serious heat and de-hydration, the college, and probably its insurance agent," she smiled briefly, "insist on that break from twelve to twelve-thirty and that work stop each day by three-thirty in the afternoon. After which, we will continue with some lecture time and discussion about the day's progress, but you otherwise can explore the area, socialize, catch up on your other studies," she waved her palm, "whatever you wish."

Suzy noticed Victor, a quiet student sitting on the far side of the rows of camp chairs. She and Victor were here on a partial work-study agreement, literally working for their suppers. They were to help prepare and clean up after the evening meals and generally assist Angela with camp duties. In exchange, the college had waived the per diem portion of their fees for the course.

Angela continued her presentation. "In response to a question from one of the students last night, I will not be lecturing directly about historical particularism, post-structuralism, diffusionism, or interpretive archeology in this seminar."

Two students shared a furtive glance and grateful smirks.

"So, don't expect a lot of history of archeological theory. But, we will talk about these and other approaches to archeology in the context of what we find here."

The blonde student to Suzy's left raised a hand. "What about taking showers?"

"By now, you have all found the three portable toilets located along the ridge behind me. There is a portable shower facility a few feet from those. The land-owner agreed to provide potable water for drinking and water for showering, which will be trucked in every few days, as needed and, yes, the water has arrived so you can take a very short shower tonight."

A few snide remarks about body odor rippled through the students.

"We'll have enough, but please conserve where you can, as it's not easy to get fresh water into here."

A student sitting behind Suzy asked, "What hap-pens to anything we find here?"

"Everything belongs to the landowner. The college will document its provenance, its exact place of origin and orientation to other features, and may offer to pur-chase items, but they belong to a private owner." Angela looked around. "Which brings me to the owner's repre-sentatives. There are three gentlemen who have the large tents by the ridge over there," she pointed, "close to an old airplane hangar, that upside-down, bowl-shaped thing. These guys are hauling the water in, helping to catalogue any finds, and providing some security."

Suzy squinted at Angela. "Security?"

"I know, I think the owner is being a bit paranoid, myself. But theft of artifacts has been known to happen, even at legitimate digs like ours. There's always been a black market for some of these things, unfortunately."

A thin man in a red baseball cap wandered into Suzy's view, a bolt-action rifle strapped to his shoulder. His boots scraped casually across the dirt but his marbled eyes focused intently on each student as he seemed to assess their prowess, one by one. He stared at Suzy for a moment, his thoughts intent but hidden, and resumed his stroll toward Ghost Creek.

"So, we just stay clear of them?" Bruce shifted on his stool.

"Please cooperate with them, as they are the owner's representatives. They are just doing their jobs, and they are supporting our efforts here."

Suzy glanced at Angela, who'd been watching Suzy stare at the man with the rifle over his shoulder.

"Everett," she began, looking back to the rest of the students, "is the owner's liaison with us, and he's also quite knowledgeable about Fremont culture. The style and design of Fremont pottery is a specific interest of his. He will be interested in our progress and may help us record and protect anything we find."

"Luke," she pointed toward the back of the man with the rifle, "is kind of a jack of all trades, and he works for Everett. We might hear him doing some target practice out in the hills or behind the hangar. Johnson is the guy who usually trucks in water and supplies. I don't see him right now, but he also works for Everett." Angela smiled at the group.

Suzy watched from the corner of her eye as Luke moved across the shallow creek and toward the cliff ruins beyond. She couldn't help wondering what three men on this location for two-and-a-half weeks could do to stay busy.

CHAPTER 8

Everett tossed the last of his coffee onto the dirt and set the mug aside. He pushed his wire-rimmed glasses tighter on his boyish face. A half-dozen ancient clay bowls spread across the folding table in front of him, some rather plain, some bearing zig-zag lines and squared-off spirals, black on white, designs within designs. He pulled back the corners on a series of documents in front of him, paging through, checking the forms as he went. Satisfied, he tapped them into a neat stack and put them in a folder in the file box at his feet.

Johnson walked under the canopy where Everett sat. "How's it going?" He pulled a dark cowboy hat off his head.

Everett turned in his camp chair and draped his elbow on the cloth backing. "Good. Finished another batch just now, but I've got five more to finish up this morning."

"You'll box them up when you're done?"

"Yep." Everett set his rounded glasses on the table, rubbed his eyes, and thought for a moment. Johnson wasn't terribly bright but he wasn't a lap dog, either, and he wasn't someone you wanted as an enemy. Neither was Luke. This was the first time Johnson and Luke had worked together and Everett had been wondering whether he could make them more dependent on his leadership somehow, keep the two of them from becoming friends and allies, at least until their project was done. When working with these kinds of people, it never hurt to add a layer of protection for yourself. And if he could play the two off each other a little, they'd be easier to control.

He slipped his glasses back on. "Same process we used last time?"

"Yep."

Everett clasped his hands together. "You've got a pick up today, is that right?"

Johnson ran his hand across the top of his crew-cut. He found another folding chair, moved it across from Everett, and sat. "Yeah. This is the special one we discussed earlier, with Luke."

"Right. This is the kid you know? The

delinquent?"

"Yeah." Johnson and Everett looked at each other for a moment. "They're runaways, I think. Dropouts. Headed for Los Angeles to disappear."

"Risky," Everett shook his head.

"But his girlfriend knows just what to take from the museum."

"They're just kids."

"The boy's OK…"

"We should be ready for the next deliveries in a couple of days."

"That should be enough time to handle and box up whatever Robbie and his girlfriend bring us." Johnson leaned back in his chair.

"Yeah…" Everett seemed ready to speak again but hesitated. "When do you think you'll be back with this Robbie guy?"

"I'm leaving now to go meet him. We should be back by noon."

"I'll be sure to walk the dig site with Angela this morning, make sure the students have no reason to be wandering back to our tents, or the old hangar here." He pointed behind him to the Quonset hut. "Then we'll do it after you get back with Robbie."

"Sure."

"I need to say something to you, though." Everett knew how to manage a pair of intellectual lightweights like Johnson and Luke. He looked around, glanced beyond the canopy, and leaned closer to his companion.

"I'm a little worried about Luke, to be honest with you. He gets, well, unsettled from time to time. Treats that scarecrow like its human and talks about ghosts in the ruins, that kind of nonsense. It's eroding some of my trust, I must say."

"I think he'll be fine. He's an odd one, but I've come to trust him."

"Have you?" Everett said.

"Well…"

"Just be careful, OK?"

"Always."

"Good. I just wanted to get that off my chest, you know."

"Sure," Johnson said.

"It's probably nothing."

"Right."

Johnson stood and nodded toward the old air strip, and Everett followed his gaze. They watched Luke walking toward them.

"Morning, troops." Luke smiled and saluted them. "Got any coffee left?"

"Sure thing." Everett pointed to a pump action thermos. "Still hot." He and Johnson glanced at each other.

"Catch you guys later…" Johnson turned and walked toward the pickup truck near the hangar.

"Have a seat," Everett pointed to the chair Johnson had used.

"Thanks, I think I will." Luke removed his Winchester 30.06 and leaned it gently against the table. He found an empty mug, filled it with black coffee, and sat across from Everett.

"It's getting hotter every day, out here," Everett remarked. "I hope you're drinking enough water…" He watched Johnson climb into the truck a few yards away.

"Oh, sure." Luke patted a small water bottle clipped to his belt.

The engine roared to life, and Johnson pulled away from the camp and onto the dirt road.

"Things going OK? Everything around the site secure?" Everett leaned forward.

"Yes, indeed. It's kind of like minding sheep, you know. Those students stay pretty close together most of the day. Sometimes, a couple wander up to the ruins or down along the creek. But mostly, I can keep track of 'em all."

"Good work, Luke, really good work."

Luke smiled.

"And you're ready for the job this afternoon?"

"Yes, sir. That special shipment is coming in, right?"

"Right. I'll make sure we're left alone this afternoon. I'll check on the students this morning."

"And that cute professor's aide, too, huh?" Luke grinned and looked at Everett from under his brow.

"Well, somebody's gotta do it..." Everett smiled proudly. "But," he leaned toward Luke, "I do just want to mention something to you. It's probably nothing, Luke, but it's been bothering me anyway and I just have to get it off my chest."

Luke's smiled drained away and he leaned closer to Everett.

"I'm just a little concerned about Johnson."

"What?"

"Well, like I say, maybe I'm off base, being paranoid, but he's made a couple little suggestions about you."

"Like what?"

"You know, just little things. Like just now, he said the special shipment will be here this afternoon and was he really trusting you to do your part of the job?"

"What!" Luke straightened.

"No, no, he just sort of hinted at it. I hope I'm wrong, Luke, but I would feel terribly guilty if I didn't tell you about my concern…"

"Well…"

"I just want to look out for you, your part in all of this is really critical."

Luke could not help but smile at the praise.

"Keep an eye on Johnson today, of all days. I know we trust each other fully," he pointed to Luke and then himself. "So let's just be aware of our surroundings, so to speak, just make sure we're all in this together," he nodded.

"Yes, yes. We're a team, here."

"Exactly."

"Don't worry about me, man. I'm on alert and ready to rock and roll."

"So glad to hear it, Luke. Hey, help me carry all this into the big blue tent, will you? It looks like rain tonight."

CHAPTER 9

A low rumble vibrated in his skull until Robbie realized that a truck was driving toward them. They'd spent the night under the stars and now a warm sort of sleep-iness slowed his thoughts like a coat of molasses. He elbowed Liz and sat up on his sleeping bag in the bed of his pickup.

A silver, dual cab truck with jacked up suspension and oversized tires made its way casually down the long dirt road, still about a half-mile away.

"Liz, he's here."

She rose on one elbow, sat up against the back window and glanced at him. Her mouth lifted in that crooked grin and she winked a gleaming eye.

He smiled quickly and scrambled to pull on his jeans and boots. When he looked at her again, she'd dressed too and brushed her hair into a tight ponytail, straight and severe, suddenly all business.

Robbie took a mouthful of water, swished it against his teeth, and spat it over the edge of his truck. He took a long swallow and capped the bottle. He clamored out, dusted off his pants and walked to the other side of his pickup, where Liz was already waiting. He and Liz stood stiffly as the silver truck pulled up next to them.

"Robbie?" A muscular man with short dark hair and reddish sideburns slid from the tall truck and walked toward them. He wore a black cowboy hat, a checkered gray and white cotton shirt, jeans, and hiking boots. A leather shoulder harness held a pistol on his left side. Mirrored sunglasses hid his eyes, but he flashed a friendly smile and offered his hand.

Robbie stepped forward and shook it.

"That's really you?" The man removed his glasses and gave Robbie an appraising look.

"Johnson, good to see you."

"You sure do remind me of your big brother." He put his sunglasses back on and turned to Liz.

"Johnson, this is my girlfriend, Liz." She shook Johnson's hand and he turned it, subtly and quickly, checking the dreamcatcher tattoo on her forearm.

"Nice to meet you." He took a half step back and

crossed his arms on his chest.

Though she'd been told this before, Robbie said to Liz: "Johnson and my brother Ed were best pals in high school." He turned back to Johnson. "Do you still see Ed these days?"

Johnson's lips tightened. "Not since last year."

"What? What happened?"

"Nothing, don't worry." He shook his head and smiled again. "What do we got?"

"Four Anasazi figurines, in perfect condition," Liz pulled her hair to the front of her shirt. "And dozens of arrowheads, knives, and scrapers, and several of those decorated plates and bowls. All from the Upper Valley Historical Center."

"Nice. With you?"

"Of course." She pointed to Robbie's pickup. "Packed in shredded newspapers and towels. Would you like to see them?"

"I know I can trust you. Right?" he looked at Robbie.

"Of course, Johnson." His eyes widened.

"Don't worry. You say you have them, you have them. And there's no sense messing up the suspension on both of our trucks. Why don't you grab the artifacts and we'll all ride in mine back to camp. We've got air conditioning and quadraphonic satellite radio. And a cooler in back."

"Sounds good, Johnson," Robbie nodded.

"You need to meet my boss, anyway. Everett will evaluate the items and make you an offer. You'll like him, don't worry."

Until then, Robbie hadn't thought to worry about it at all.

CHAPTER 10

Relic stared across the canyon, broad where it opened along the massive Colorado River, narrow as it rose to the plain where the tents were pitched. An old two-track road wound its way through the plateau to the south, its rough heritage re-worked into a smoother, dusty road used by the diggers. The nearest paved road was thirty-four miles away, the nearest supplies nearly a day's drive. A grass airstrip, seldom used, angled away from the Quonset hut. A thin man with a red cap and a rifle across his shoulder, the man he'd seen with a scarecrow, patrolled the area during the day and shared one of the big tents with the third mystery man.

The excavation seemed well-organized. Yesterday, a pickup full of water and probably food, propane, and luxuries, arrived. The truck drained water into a cistern that rested near the family-style tents, then drove back along the dirt road. An older, reddish pickup sat along the edge of the tarps, close to the pile of fresh dirt that pointed like a finger behind the Quonset hut.

The crunch of boots on gravel drew his attention to the trail below the ruins. He peered over the edge of the cliff.

"Shit on a shingle."

The rifleman in the red cap was working his way up, holding his gun harness tight against his shoulder. He was gangly, his elbows and knees jutting with each step, out and back, exaggerating his rail-thin limbs. The man stopped to catch his breath.

Relic pulled away from the edge and stood quietly, careful not to scratch his heels across the barren rock. He slung his pack onto his back and scanned the empty ruins. A rectangular building anchored the western end of the complex. Behind that, four other roofless walls were laid out, maze-like, in front of another stone structure that rose all the way to the ceiling of the cliff, three stories high. Rectangular doors, wide at the top and narrower at the bottom, stood like shadow sentries, reminiscent of petroglyph figures with broad shoulders and narrow waists.

In times of danger, his grandfather's people had climbed to the fortified homes and pulled their ladders up behind them. They'd ground shallow steps into an area on the bluff so they had one place where a person could ascend without help, if that became necessary. Hard to climb safely to the top, easy for the people to defend. But the rifleman could use those cuts in the cliff too.

Relic picked a spot at the back of the outermost structure, a place dark in shadow where he could huddle out of sight. He moved silently in that direction, listening to the rifleman grunt and strain up the slippery toe- and hand-holds.

Relic stepped gingerly over a crumbled outer wall and crossed to the doorway of a well-preserved stone room several yards from the edge of the cliff. He placed his pack in the corner and settled into a position he could keep for a long time, if need be. He could hear the rifleman reach the top of his climb and catch his breath.

Feet shuffled and twisted against the rock. Relic leaned forward and glanced outside the doorway. The man lay prone against the sandstone, rifle pointed out across the canyon below, aiming at something in the distance.

Crack! A shot echoed through the ruins like a metal drum, vibrating Relic's innards, jerking him involuntarily, making his teeth clench. He heard the slide of the bolt-action, metal on metal, as the man chambered another round.

Crack! The second shot seemed worse than the first, this quiet ruin helpless against the violence of a modern weapon. Relic kept his breathing shallow as he listened for movement, perhaps another bullet into the breach. But the air was now still and the man motionless.

Relic peered carefully out the doorway again. Rifleman placed the gun stock onto the ground and stood, watching carefully where he'd shot.

"Hell, yes, that's some real shooting," he congratulated himself. "Maybe three hundred yards," he chuckled. "Might need a new scarecrow, though. You're nothin' but a ghost of one now." He scratched his chin. "But I guess we're all ghosts sooner or later, so…what's the difference? It's all scarecrows into ghosts."

Rifleman lifted his red cap, rubbed his scalp, and returned the hat to his head. He turned slowly to examine the ruins, scanning the ancient homes with a hint of suspicion.

"Ghost House…" he whispered. He gazed into the third-story window of the rear tower and squared his shoulders toward it. He took a tentative step forward and Relic could see the man's urge to investigate, but then he glanced at his watch. "Later," he declared. The man replaced his feet where he'd begun, still several yards away from the ruins. He turned toward the dark doorway next to Relic, then swung slowly and directly to the room where Relic hid.

Relic didn't know whether moving out of the line of sight now would give him away, so he held his breath, still as the air before a storm, staring at the shooter from ancient shadows. Rifleman's eyes were watery blue marbles, his face unshaven and gaunt, his expression deadpan. He stared directly into Relic's face.

A throaty growl of distant thunder seemed to wake the man from a trance. He shook his head and looked at his watch again. Relic moved his face behind the stone ruin and released a slow breath. Moments later, he heard the man scrambling over rock and dared to take another look beyond the wall.

He heard Rifleman working his way backwards down the old steps carved into the cliff, sliding one leg down, then the other, careful to keep his grip.

Relic rose slowly from hiding and went quietly to the east tower, a spot in the ruins that let him see the flats and the distant camp. He peered through his binoculars and found what was left of the strange scarecrow, its stiff form shot in two, legs splayed in the dust, chest and head twisted away, splintered into pieces. Rifleman's target.

Relic scanned the ground farther away, across the little creek and to the south. A silver pickup barreled down the dirt road, dust rising from its tires, turning toward the site. Relic adjusted his binoculars and watched as the truck stopped near the larger tents. A husky man stepped from the driver's side and put a cowboy hat on his head.

A thin girl emerged from the back and another man, young and skinny, slid from the front cab. The men lifted duffle bags from the truck bed and they all walked beneath the tarps strung against the hangar and disappeared. The man in the red cap strode into view below the cliffs, making his way toward the tents, rifle on his shoulder. Relic put his binoculars away.

Rain clouds, dark as night, piled high on themselves on the western rim and crackled.

CHAPTER 11

Luke wound his way along one of the light trails leading from the student's camp to the bigger tents near the old Quonset hut. He pulled the rifle higher on his shoulder.

His stomach clutched at his experience at the pueblo ruins, up on the cliff. Had he really seen a pair of eyes in one of the houses, a ghost of that place? Yes, he had. The more he thought about it, the more certain he was, but just when he'd nearly convinced himself, he began to doubt it again too. Damn it. He should have stayed and gone into the stone ruins. Now, the sighting was going to bother him with no end. He was going to have to go up there again and search each one of those ruins, listen for the sounds of moving spirits, find out if the name of the place was based on something real or something imagined.

He heard Everett's voice and looked up. Everett

led a teenaged guy and girl to the other side of the hut and around the corner, behind the old hangar.

He saw Johnson walking away from them, toward his pickup truck. Johnson watched Luke intently for a moment, then nodded toward the back of the hut. Luke nodded in reply and made his way toward Everett and the delinquents.

****

"What do we have here?"

Johnson had set up a folding table behind the Quonset hut for the meeting and introduced Robbie and Liz to Everett. Then Johnson left to keep an eye on the dig site, in case any students decided to wander toward the meeting. Everett had introduced Luke when he'd arrived, then Luke leaned on the edge of the old hangar and cleaned the dirt from under his fingernails.

Everett eyed the duffle bags and waved at Robbie to open them onto the table.

"Sure, Mister…?"

"Call me Everett."

"Right." Robbie unzipped the closest bag and began removing loose rags and newspapers that protected the artifacts.

"No, Robbie," Liz moved forward and touched his arm. "Show him the figurines first…"

"Oh, right." He reached for another duffle.

"We have bowls and other pottery, chert knives, all kinds of other tools, but we also have something really special to show you…" Liz's lopsided smile rose high at the edges, her speckled eyes glistened.

With both hands, Robbie lifted a bundle of terry-cloth and laid it on the table. Carefully, he removed the outer layer and untied an inner cloth composed of four separate pockets. He spread it flat and reached inside the first sleeve, pulling from it a pale clay figure of a man with markings showing hair on its head, slashes for eyes, etchings for its arms, legs, and garb. Inlaid pieces of shell shimmered along its waist. Circling lines depicted boots on its feet.

Everett leaned closer to look.

"Beautiful, isn't it?" Liz asked. "Three more of them too, look like they're a family."

Everett tried to repress his surprise. These were truly rare and valuable. He took a step back and looked to the sky for a moment, choosing his words.

"Beautiful, indeed, Liz… Robbie." He nodded. "Very nice. These kinds of figurines go for five, maybe even six thousand dollars a piece on the black market."

Liz's eyes quickly matched the storm above them. "Bullshit."

"What?" Everett stepped back.

"That's bullshit. These are worth thirty-five thousand a piece and, as a set, they're worth two hundred thousand."

"Now wait just a minute, young lady." Everett felt the heat rise in his cheeks. "I've been in this business for years and I know what these are worth on the market."

"Wrap them back up, Robbie!" She spun her fingers in the air.

Robbie glanced at her, his eyes wide.

"What are you doing?" Everett asked.

"Leaving…" Liz moved toward Robbie.

"Hey, we've all worked hard to get to this place. We need to at least try to make a deal…" Everett spread his arms.

"Two hundred thousand, that's the price." Liz straightened her back.

"Look, they're worth maybe twenty-four thousand. As a set, well, maybe thirty…" Everett gave her his best smile and a quick shrug of his shoulders. "Maybe if we add the rest of what you have, we could get to fifty…"

"Wrap them up, Robbie, we're out of here."

Damn it all. Everett stared at Liz's face, hardened as the rocks around them. These kids were more immature, more wet behind the ears, than he'd expected.

Liz motioned toward the figurines and Robbie slid the one they'd examined back into its sleeve.

"Where else are you going to go with these?" Everett circled his arms in the air. "You think you can find just anyone to buy these from you? You can walk away from fifty thousand dollars?"

Robbie looked to Liz, a quiet plea in his eyes.

Everett turned toward Robbie. "You can make a helluva start for yourselves with fifty thousand dollars, son. It's a bucket load of cash… And it's without any more risk for the two of you."

Robbie squinted at the ground, and Everett pressed him. "You sell to us, you're all done, out of it, clean as a whistle. You keep these figurines, well, these are some serious contraband, and the FBI is searching for them right now, I can guarantee it. You want the FBI to find you guys with those artifacts in your back pocket?"

Robbie seemed to be considering the point.

"You sell to us, you're out clean, right now." Everett's hands slashed the air.

Liz shook her head at Everett. "Robbie's brother

can get us a way better price. And we'll be done with it all by next week."

Well, shit, Everett thought, dropping his hands to his side. Johnson said this Robbie guy was all right, but his bitch of a girlfriend was hell on steroids. Though she wasn't wrong about the value of the artifacts...

"Listen, Liz, think this through. We've got serious connections here, to the underground market. We've worked for years to develop this, we've got the best retail around, but you," he pointed to her, "and me," he pointed at himself, "we're working wholesale, you know? Our buyer has to make a profit, right?"

Liz's lips hardened.

"That's just how business works, right?"

She folded her arms across her chest. Robbie finished wrapping the figurines and began placing them back into the duffle bag.

Damn it. Everett wasn't getting anywhere with Liz. He put his forehead in his hand and released a sigh. "Look, what if we got you closer to one hundred thousand? What if we could do that?"

Liz blinked.

"It's not ideal for you, certainly not ideal for us. We'll have to sell like a fiend to get any profit on this..."

She tapped her boot against the ground.

"Listen," Everett turned to Luke, then back to her. "Let me talk with my colleagues for a minute. What harm is there in that? You're pushing us to our limit here, and I need a moment to confer…"

Liz glanced at the ground. "Sure. But we're not waiting all day."

Everett raised his hands toward her. "Right, right. Just…let me see if there's any way to make a deal today or not. I'll be back." He walked to Luke and pulled him along the side of the old hangar. They moved into the open archway and to the side of an aging airplane.

"What in damnation?" Everett slapped his thigh. "What did Johnson bring us, the delinquents from hell?" He paced under the wing. "Where is Johnson's tiny, tiny, little brain?"

"He thought we could trust the kid."

Luke watched Everett raise and lower his arms, trashing some invisible foe.

"Shit, shit, shit."

"Do we even have a hundred thousand dollars?" Luke asked.

"Not here, no, we barely have half of that. We've spent most of our cash on hand."

"Maybe we tell them that, tell them they'll have to wait for us to get the rest of the money." Luke shifted the rifle on his shoulder.

"Hell, no. We're not paying those punks two hundred, one hundred, even fifty thousand…" Everett rested his hand on a strut below the airplane wing and thought.

If he couldn't sweet talk Liz, and he couldn't reason with her, there was no deal to be had. But having them go to someone else? No matter who he was, Robbie's brother wasn't going to get them a better deal, so they'd be shopping those figurines all over the place. A pair of teenagers? If they got caught – when they got caught – they'd tell the police all about him and Luke and Johnson and how they'd tried to "cheat" them out of a fair deal. And now, thanks to Johnson, they'd tell the FBI right where the camp is located. Liz might seem pretty tough, but Robbie would fold in a flash. Shit.

After a moment, Everett straightened. "These figurines could be our biggest score. They're worth every penny that bitch wants."

Luke's eyebrow rose.

"We can get a hundred fifty thousand for them."

"So…what do we do, boss?"

"Didn't Johnson say Robbie's older brother tried to rat him out once?"

Luke nodded.

"So, Johnson could give a shit what happens to them, right? And didn't he say those kids were runaways? Eloping to L.A. or some such craziness?"

"Yeah, I think he did."

"So, who would miss them if they disappeared?"

CHAPTER 12

Luke made his way under the tarps, between the hangar and the big tents. Behind them rose a mound of dirt left there years ago, probably from the time the airstrip was levelled. The ground stretched from the back of the hut, finger-like, to a natural bank of rock, a low ridge that ran north and south.

Staying on the far side of the dirt, Luke found his way to the ridge and climbed loose rock to the top, about sixteen feet high. From there, he could easily see the family-style tents to his left, the hangar roof in front of him, and the mound that connected the ridge with part of the hangar, to his right. He could not see over the dirt, but Everett's voice carried clearly through the air. Everett had rejoined Robbie and Liz behind the old Quonset hut.

"Listen, Liz, we might have a solution here…"

"The dolls alone are worth two hundred thousand…"

"Sure, let's agree on that. But that's retail, Liz…"

Luke worked his way toward them, placing his feet quietly along the rocks.

"Bullshit." Luke heard the resolve in the girl's voice.

"Look, let's just say that everything you've brought here today is worth two hundred thousand, just for argument." Everett's words were calm, matter of fact.

"OK…"

Luke peered ahead and saw the three of them well below him, about forty yards away.

"That's street value, Liz. Retail. We sell to the dealer. He gets retail, not us. To make it worth his while, we have to sell two hundred thousand worth of artifacts to him for one hundred thousand, right?" Everett spread his arms. "He has to make something, right?"

Liz nodded reluctantly.

Luke moved two feet closer. He found a level stone and lowered himself to the ground.

"OK. So if we sell to him for one hundred thousand, we have to make something too, right?" Everett asked.

Robbie shifted from one foot to the next but

said nothing.

Everett moved slowly toward the rear of the hangar, squarely facing Luke's position.

"We should make more than one hundred thousand." Liz pointed a finger at Everett.

"And that's why we're prepared to offer you one hundred and twenty-five, for the whole lot."

Liz looked at Robbie, who nodded. "What do you think?" he asked her.

She turned back to Everett. "One hundred fifty thousand, that's it." She folded her arms across her chest again.

Luke moved the Winchester off of his shoulder and nestled into position. The sun dipped below western clouds, muting its harsh glare across the canyon.

Everett stared at the ground and shook his head. "Look, Liz, Robbie, I like you guys and you're friends of Johnson's… Maybe we could do a hundred thirty thousand." He looked up at them and glanced quickly over their heads, at Luke.

Liz turned to Robbie and whispered in his ear. Robbie nodded, stopped a moment, and nodded again.

"We'll go to one-forty, but that's it. No lower." Her voice was friendly, but firm.

"Shit, you guys, you are driving a hard bargain

here." Everett held his chin in his hand for a moment. "We wouldn't do this for anyone but a friend of Johnson's, but… OK. We have a deal."

Liz and Robbie relaxed immediately and they all shook hands.

"Thanks, Everett. Good dealing with you," Liz said.

"OK then. We have the cash here, but it's in a safe location. It will take us about fifteen minutes to get it all together. If you can hang out here, I'll bring you a couple of cold brews while you wait." Everett glanced toward the hangar. "As you can see, we're sharing this place with a bunch of college students."

Liz narrowed her eyes. "Yeah, why?"

"Good cover for the operation. But we also can't do too much out in the open."

"Sure, sure, we get it," Robbie held up his palms. "Gotta be careful here."

Everett nodded. "Be back shortly with some beers." He turned and walked around the Quonset hut and out of view.

Liz and Robbie turned to each other and embraced. Two skinny scarecrows, Luke thought, two wooden targets tangled together. Scarecrow to ghost, each one of them, just like the other scarecrow, just like any other target practice. But worth a hundred fifty thousand in cash.

Two shots echoed across the canyon in quick succession.

CHAPTER 13

An early morning sun smeared its rich, honey glow through the windows and across the inner office walls. Owen glanced at a glare on the glass then looked down at the government-gray carpet. He gripped a National Park Service cap in his hands.

"Look, I get it…" District Ranger Mary Roselli tapped her pencil on an empty mug with a *Canyonlands* logo. "We hear about a string of museum thefts and we'd all like to get more involved. If our guess is right, the artifacts have already been sold on the black market and are long gone from Utah. But we don't know for sure. So right now, our role is important, but limited. We need to keep an eye out for anything unusual on federal lands." She pushed away from the desk and looked up at Owen, her brown eyes tense.

"I guess that's right." He shifted his weight from

one foot to the other.

Roselli crossed her arms. "I need you to go with a guy named Thomas Morris to a spot on Ghost Creek. There's a long dirt road into there and some tight side-canyons that make for good hiding places. You'll check on any vehicles and any activity, make sure no one is on federal land without a permit."

"Yes, ma'am."

"It'll be a long day, so you can go home for the three day weekend whenever you are done with Thomas. If you have nothing to report, we can talk again on Monday."

"Thanks."

She placed her hands on the sides of her chair. "You're getting into a law enforcement career, long term, am I right?" Her left brow rose with the question.

'Well,' he fiddled with his NPS-issued smartphone holster. Probation Officer Pete had encouraged him to tell the Park Service he was interested in law enforcement in the hope it would help him advance to a permanent position back in Virginia. He'd said it again to Ranger Roselli during his telephone interview, but now that he was here with her, face to face, it felt uncomfortable, a statement more from his old juvenile officer than from himself.

"This falls right into that objective, Owen. It's more than just an overview today. Think of it as an inspection, a bit of an investigation, even. We're spread awful thin, you know, and your trip will cover a good piece of territory."

He nodded.

"There's a private dig going on there at Ghost Creek, through some college or other. Talk to the dig 'boss.' Look around a little. There are cliff dwellings across the creek, on government land, so wander over there if you like and look for signs of any recent human activity, any trespassing. Remember your training. If you find anything out of place, be safe about it. Tell Thomas and the two of you fly on home and report it to me."

"Fly?"

"It's a single engine, a Cessna 172. There's a grass airstrip near the creek."

Owen swallowed. "Who's Thomas, again?"

"He's a private contractor, a pilot, but he's done this with our rangers lots of times. He'll show you the ropes."

"Yes, ma'am." He glanced out the window behind her desk. Green grass stretched from the building to the NPS sign at the edge of a small parking space.

"And it should be smooth flying today… Winds look good after last night's rain." A heavy storm had battered lands to the north and swept through the ranger station in the early morning hours, shaking the rooftops, cooling the air.

"Yes, I suppose so."

"Good. Bill will get you your standard gear. Water, snacks, flares. And he'll point you toward the airport, where Thomas will be waiting. We're counting on you."

"Thanks," Owen nodded. He'd only been on assignment here for ten days, but he knew when Ranger Roselli was done talking and she was not one for idle chat. He turned and marched from her office, wondering just what he'd gotten himself into.

He checked the maps posted in the hall, running his finger from Ghost Creek ruins along the dotted line marking the dirt road to the highway and back again, acting like he knew what he was doing. He gathered his gear and Bill directed him toward a tin hangar about three hundred yards behind the Park Service offices, adjacent to a small, public airstrip.

He stood for a moment and looked out across the field, wondering about the Cessna. And whether a temporary summer intern could qualify for any of that reward money.

CHAPTER 14

Owen finished checking his cell phone for messages and walked across the field toward the airport.

The morning sun lit a red rock mesa to the distant north, a rough beard of sage on its unshaven face. Behind that rose a layer of sharp cliffs, pink in the light, framed in the baby blue of a day still fresh on the horizon.

How alien it all seemed to him, here in the high desert. He missed the moist layer of haze on the landscape, the wrinkled blankets of spinach-colored hills, the maples, pines, thickets of wine berries, bushes, and weeds dense as a darkened jungle. The land seemed emptier here, the air thinner, dry as a cracker, hard to swallow.

He thought about Lydia, who he'd met at Williamsburg some months ago. They'd both headed for the only empty picnic table at the lunch station, she in her colonial bonnet and he in his dark uniform. They'd met at noon three more times after that, chicken sandwiches and sliced apples, before he'd worked up the nerve to ask her to supper. For their third date, she invited him to a family dinner. Her father, a retired security chief, probed his intentions and ambitions, not terribly subtle. He'd talked about being the officer in charge, the responsibility of authority, the mantle of manhood. He'd slapped Owen on the back, reminding him that a young man has to stay grounded to succeed, focused on his career. Flights of fancy weren't a path to self-respect, he'd said. Putting on the work-harness, ignoring distractions, those were part of adult life, words he'd heard as a child whenever he rattled on about time travel, flying through space, deep-sea monsters. Like Probation Officer Pete, Lydia's father encouraged Owen to consider a life in law enforcement. Lydia seemed pretty impressed with the idea too, but, cute as she was, Owen was not so sure.

And now, hell and away from Lydia and family and school mates, plays and movies and concerts, he had only work to busy himself with during the day and a thin bunk to sit on at night. Thank god for his smartphone. He could play games, catch national news, watch funny videos on YouTube. His connection to civilization.

Owen refocused and walked closer to the tarmac. A lanky man in a red shirt and white baseball cap stepped around a small plane, inspecting hinges and cables on the ailerons, horizontal, and tail. The man climbed onto a strut and checked fluids in the wings – must be the gasoline, Owen realized. The man was checking the tires, kicking them gently, when Owen arrived.

"You must be Thomas..."

"You must be Owen." The man turned and offered his hand. His smile, broad and genuine, tightened his cheeks and crinkled his eyes.

"Got her all ready?"

"Yep. Great day for a flight." Thomas turned back to the Cessna. "Ever fly in one of these?"

"No." Owen examined the propeller, the sleek fuselage, the curved tail. "But I flew in an old tail-dragger once." He'd been fourteen years old, at a county fair near Oxford, airplane rides ten dollars a pop, and he'd begged his mother to let him fly. They went only once around the grass strip but the feel of it had lasted for years, a weightlessness and exhilaration he'd never forget.

"Well, we have thirty-six gallons useable." Thomas

ran his fingers along the edge of the propeller. "Plenty for this trip."

Owen nodded.

"Only once?" Thomas looked at him, his question light-hearted.

"I've thought about taking lessons, but…it's expensive and of course I'm working, and I've just never had the time…" These were valid points and most people accepted them at face value but, in front of Thomas, they sounded a little like excuses.

"Well, it's a great day, so let's get going."

Something flittered in Owen's stomach.

CHAPTER 15

Owen tossed his gear in the back, slid into the co-pilot seat, and put on the headset. Thomas hopped into the pilot seat and they both buckled in, shoulders touching in the tight cockpit.

Thomas pumped a metal rod with a knob on the end. "This is the throttle, Owen. Like most planes, the pilot and co-pilot each have their own set of pedals for turning the front wheel when on the taxiway and the tail when in the air, and each have their own yoke, too," he pointed at them, "connected together, for climbing, descending, or rolling the wings left or right. Important controls like the throttle and flaps are on the dash between the pilot and co-pilot, within easy reach of either."

Owen nodded.

"Clear prop!" Thomas turned the key and

pumped more fuel into the carburetor, coaxing the engine into a steady rumble. Owen's bones vibrated in unison with the metal frame. The propeller became a translucent blur and Thomas turned on the radio and GPS. He seemed to run through a mental checklist, adjusting the dials on various instruments on the panel.

Satisfied, Thomas rolled gently to the end of the pavement and double-checked the compass marking for Ghost Creek. The wind sock hung limply at mid-field, exhausted after the velocity of the overnight storm. He announced his departure over the radio, revved the engine full throttle, and accelerated until the plane lifted from the ground and carried them into the blue morning sky.

They rose slowly about 500 feet and Thomas turned them gently south.

"If you'd like to learn a little, I've been a flight instructor for six years now…" Thomas smiled.

Owen looked at the array of puzzling instruments. Why not a quick lecture? "Sure."

"Best way to learn is to jump right in, get a feel for it. Here," Thomas released the yoke. "You take it for a while."

What?

The Cessna dipped slowly to the right.

Owen reached forward quickly and leveled the plane. He tried to level his breathing too.

"Let's go higher and practice a slow-speed stall. They're fun. It's the same maneuver you make right as you land, and if you decide to take lessons, you'll need to know how to do it."

"Sure." But Owen was not sure at all. This was not his job, he'd had no training, it was dangerous, he couldn't do it, Ranger Roselli would blow a gasket if she found out. But Thomas had his hands folded in his lap, determined not to help. So Owen pushed gently forward on the yoke, just a little, feeling the nose of the aircraft dip, then pulled it back, watching it rise again. He twisted the yoke left, then right, feeling the wings angle down and up with each move. He glanced nervously at Thomas, who smiled.

"You're not gonna just fall out of the sky, you know."

Owen chuckled nervously and looked out the front window, the distant mesa growing larger.

"Check your altitude and speed."

Owen watched the altimeter rise to nearly 6,000 feet, about 2,000 feet above the ground, and checked their speed, the needle wavering at 92 miles per hour.

"I'm going to throttle back." Thomas reduced

the power dramatically. "Now, pull back on the yoke until the stall warning screams. Do your best to keep the wings level, but don't sweat it. I'll take the yoke back if I need to."

Owen took a quick breath, centered himself in his seat and pulled the yoke steadily toward his chest, their view out the front window now filled only with sky as they pointed toward the heavens, the stall warning whining its alarm louder and louder, the wings more and more difficult to keep level, sweat running down Owen's armpits even in the cool morning air.

"Nice." Thomas retook control of the yoke and pushed it forward, leveling the plane with the horizon and silencing the stall alarm. "Thing is, 172s don't want to stall, hard as you try. They practically fly themselves." He grinned widely and nodded at Owen.

Fly themselves? Owen wondered and stared back at Thomas. Maybe for you…

"Remember, engine power gets you higher, but just pointing the nose up, without power, gets you a stall, and that can get you into a tailspin. Could ruin your day." He flashed a smile at Owen. "But keep your speed about eighty miles an hour and you have a controlled glide, a controlled landing closer to sixty."

"Got it." Owen glanced at the airspeed needle.

Thomas seemed to have provided his lesson for the day and they flew on in silence, studying the ground below them. Owen watched out the window, re-living the tug of the yoke, the sound of the stall alarm, the high angle and soft float of the plane as it descended.

Turning northwest, then east again, they saw a dried-out riverbed where the muscled flow had circled a horseshoe bend until, eons ago, it met itself coming and going and abandoned the island of rock to the desert winds. From above, the land looked as furrowed as a crumpled rug and raw as sandpaper, tall spires like pencils of rock, deep canyons a summer sandbox carved with the flow of a garden hose. Ribbons of living green hugged tightly against the massive Colorado River as it wound slowly through the dry mesas and sheer cliffs, erosions and uplifts on a scale of size and time too vast for human minds to grasp. He stared at it all, the sound of the engine washing away his sense of perspective.

"There." Thomas pointed at a narrow landing strip near a building backed against a low ridge, tarps and tents in one area and other tents maybe forty yards away, along a thin strip of green that Owen guessed was nurtured by a creek.

Thomas reduced all power and glided down toward the dirt strip, lined up for final approach, and eased gently through the air. As they grew close, he pulled the yoke back until the stall warning screeched and the tires squealed and they bounced and jostled to a stop. Thomas revved the engine and turned the plane around, lining up for takeoff whenever they were ready to leave.

CHAPTER 16

The woman in the broad straw hat introduced herself as Angela Lazarus, aide in charge of the archeological dig on the southern side of Ghost Creek. She laid a single blonde braid over her shoulder and hooked her thumbs in her cargo pants.

"And this is Suzy," she pointed to a younger woman by her side, "one of our students."

Suzy's eyes scanned Thomas quickly, met Owen's gaze and flashed for a second, then looked to the ground. Her expression startled him a bit, her intense brown eyes glistening and calming so quickly he may have imagined it. Her skin had begun to tan from the desert sun, her long, dark hair bleached a bit lighter on the ends. She glanced up again, smiled, and nodded at them both. "Is that a Cessna 172?"

"Yep," Thomas smiled. "You fly?"

"Some. With my grandpa."

"What brings you to these distant parts?" Angela asked.

"Routine check by the Park Service, ma'am. I'm Thomas Morris, a part-time contractor with the service, but please call me Thomas, and this is Owen."

A short, fit man with round spectacles and a blue baseball cap strode to the group, hand outstretched.

"Everett Bonache, glad to meet you."

Owen and Thomas repeated their names and shook hands with Everett, who nodded a greeting to Angela and Suzy. "What precipitates a visit from our fine federal friends?"

"I was telling Ms. Lazarus, here, we're just here for a routine check." Thomas looked toward the dig.

"Well, check away, officer." Everett looked at Owen like he was sizing up a pork chop. "What can we do to help?"

Thomas turned back to Angela. "We also want to warn you about a recent museum robbery at Upper Valley. The thieves got away with valuable artifacts we suspect are part of a flow of artifacts into the black market."

"We've seen nothing suspicious here, officer." Angela narrowed her eyes.

"No thefts, nothing missing from your dig?"

"No, of course not. We keep meticulous records and photographs." She glanced at Everett.

He cleared his throat. "I represent the landowner. She's signed a lease with the Wyndotte College to undertake the dig and, Angela's right, we verify any finds and photograph, mark, and log them." He smiled a row of ice-white teeth.

"Glad to hear it," Thomas nodded.

"I have to say, gentlemen, I'm a bit confused here. I mean, we're on private land. Federal property starts on the other side of Ghost Creek." Everett watched them from under his brow. "I mean, technically, you're trespassing here…"

Thomas started to reply.

"But no, no," Everett jumped in, "You're very welcome, look around all you like, check our paperwork, I'm just saying…" he spread his arms.

"I get your point, Mr. Bonache, and we appreciate your cooperation. I'd like to spend a bit of time with Ms. Lazarus, here--"

"Call me Angela."

"…so I can fill out my report and verify that the dig you're conducting is on private land only, and, also, that you've had no problems with missing artifacts or any other kinds of issues."

Angela smiled flirtatiously and waved Thomas to come closer. "Follow me. I'll get you a copy of our lease with the owner and show you all around the dig. Come on, Suzy, let's give this man a guided tour."

Thomas nodded an approval to Owen and walked away with Angela and Suzy.

"Owen…" Everett looked at him and then smiled, an afterthought. "Why don't you come with me and we'll have a nice cold drink in the shade."

Everett turned and Owen followed him toward two large, family-style tents.

"The college provided a nice lease bonus and funds for us to stay here and monitor the site." Everett waved toward the dig. "So, we provide water and supplies. The water, we have to haul about every four days, depending on use, so we have a truck for that…" Owen began to lose the content of Everett's narrative, his voice turning into background noise.

"Wait." Owen pointed to the cliffs above the boxelders that lined the creek. "Is that a set of old ruins, way up there?" he pointed. Empty doorways stared out across the canyon, their sharp, straight lines in contrast with the curving cliffs and merging horizons.

"Right. That's Ghost House Ruins, they call

them, beyond the creek over there." Everett stopped and looked in their direction. "That's federal land over there, which of course you know, so we stay clear of that. Besides," he chuckled, "they're haunted, you know." He looked at Owen, checking his reaction.

"Right," Owen's voice was matter of fact.

"Well," Everett shrugged, "that's what Luke says. He's another member of our team. He patrols around here, keeps an eye on things and does his target practice about every day. Says it helps keep the mountain lions away."

"Mountain lions…"

"Yep. We haven't seen any here, but Luke swears that's because he patrols the place." Everett shrugged. "Anyway, the owner likes the guy and he's a good hand to have around. Come on, let's get that cold drink."

Owen turned. From the corner of his eye, he saw a tall, thin man in a red cap and rifle on his shoulder move past the tents and out of view. Luke, he presumed.

As they approached the campsite, Owen could see deeper into the shadows of the old Quonset hut and the shape of an airplane inside.

"You've got a plane here?"

"The owner does. Don't know if still flies, don't think it's been flown for years." Everett pointed to two camp chairs in the shade. "You know what… Owen, is it?"

Owen nodded.

"Have a seat. There's a cooler between the chairs. Help yourself. I see my friend Luke wants a word with me. I won't be a minute." Everett strode away purposefully, toward where Owen had seen the rifleman.

Owen stood for a moment, staring at the shadowed form of an airplane in the old hangar and decided to see what was there. He was here to investigate, after all.

He walked into the shade of the Quonset hut and examined the aircraft. He didn't know much, but this one appeared to be old school, maybe from the 1940s. A faded "Aeronca" insignia was painted behind the engine cowling. The wings and fuselage were covered in fabric, a faded lemon-yellow, strands of threadbare cloth hung loose along the door. But the tires were tight with air, a fuel gauge on the dash showed it was half-full of gasoline. Maybe the owner was restoring it, a flying antique.

The rest of the space was empty but for two fifty-gallon drums, a wooden stool, and what looked like an old lawnmower. He shuffled through the old hangar and back into the sunlight.

He could still see the pueblo ruins from here and wondered if he would have the chance to see some of those places up close. He wound around the edge of the hangar and toward a low ridge of loose dirt that ran at an angle from a rock face behind the camp. Rivulets from last night's storm had washed away sections of the soil. His mind wandered as he strolled along the bank of roof-high dirt to the end of it. He moved along the other side, glancing at the cliff and clear sky beyond, then turned to make his way back to the camp.

There, directly before him in the eroded dirt, rose a statue of an arm, a dreamcatcher tattooed below the wrist. Fingers, gray and stiff, shivered in the breeze and trembled more deeply, too, at the elbow.

Mannequin fingers, he thought at first. Then he realized what they really were.

CHAPTER 17

Owen thought his heart had completely halted, and it had, for just a second, and then it began a pounding, deep and strained, pumping blood through his temple in spurts then galloping quickly, flushing his cheeks.

Holy flying eff.

He sucked a shallow breath of air, pulled his gaze from the dead arm, and looked back the way he'd come. From this perspective, the arm was well-hidden on the backside of the long pile of dirt, tucked close to the low rock face and well out of view from the hangar and the tents beyond. Last night's heavy storm had flushed loose soil from the canyon slopes and probably from the body, too. He tried not to look back at the fragile hand, but he couldn't help himself. Skin shriveled against the tiny bones, stiff leather holding the assembly of joints together, keeping the fingers pointed in confusing, haphazard directions, their owner not sure which way to go. Red nail polish added a cheap party flare, a celebration completely out of place.

Holy eff. Hold it together, he told himself, get back to camp and pretend he'd never seen it. Tell Thomas. No one else. Someone here could have killed this girl, must have killed her. Why? What had happened here?

He turned his eyes to his feet and shuffled across the ground, moving to the edge of the pile of dirt. He peered around the mound and saw the edge of the hangar and the back of the tents. No one seemed to be around, so he hustled away from the dirt, across the hard-packed surface, and into the hangar. He went to the yellow plane again and leaned on the right strut, his breath still shallow and labored.

Owen looked beyond the hangar to the field outside and the Cessna waiting for them. Where was Thomas?

"Did you get that cold drink?"

Panic charged through his brain, a devil's hot wire crackling from one ear to the other. His head jerked toward the front of the plane and he clamped his hands tightly on the strut. Everett's question was smooth but – was there an undertone in his voice?

Owen managed to force a breath.

"No…" he patted the wing support, glanced at Everett, then spoke to the plane itself, too nervous to look at the man again. Squeezing the strut helped him to focus. "I got sidetracked by this old Aeronca. What year is it, do you know?"

"1946, I'm told."

"Oh."

"Are you a pilot?" Everett moved out of the sunlight and into the shade of the hangar. Owen knew the man could see him better now.

"No, no, I'm not. Tried to take some lessons, but…" He struggled to keep his thoughts on the aircraft, away from what he'd discovered. "Just look at this panel, the instrument panel," he pointed. "Not hardly any instruments here, though. It's all metal, too, like the dashboards on old cars." He kept his eyes on the cockpit, still reluctant to look directly at Everett.

"Yeah, I've looked it over myself." Everett's voice seemed more normal now, more conversational. "The owner has a friend who came out here a couple of days ago. He's restoring the old bird, but I don't know how far he's gotten. The fabric looks like a stiff breeze would pull it off." He ran his hand across the edge of the wing opposite Owen. "You wouldn't catch me flying in this death trap." Everett wandered away from the plane, plucked a long blade of grass from the ground and began to twist it absentmindedly.

"Yeah, the cloth on this one needs completely replaced." Owen tried to sound like an authority on the subject and felt his nerves calm a little as he spoke. He ducked under the wing and walked into the sunlight. "Seen my boss?"

"I think he's about done," Everett pointed toward the tents along Ghost Creek. Thomas and Angela were walking slowly back toward the Cessna. Angela was explaining something, Thomas nodding.

"Well, it was nice meeting you." Everett moved quickly toward Owen and offered his hand, his smile show-room friendly, his shake cold and curt.

"Yes. Nice meeting you, too." Owen made eye contact briefly and turned back toward the Cessna. "Better get going."

"I guess we'll get that cold drink another time," Everett spoke under his breath.

Owen strode toward the rented Park Service plane, muscle memory moving his legs, thoughts flowing back to that tortured hand, its ragged movement in the breeze. He tried to be nonchalant about getting the hell out of there. Angela and Thomas came closer to the Cessna.

"Got what we need?" Owen asked Thomas.

Thomas looked up. "Yep. Thanks for the tour and good luck to you," he said to Angela. He shook hands with her and Everett and turned back to the plane.

Owen did not wait to be told to climb in. He adjusted his seatbelt, put the headset on, and waited. Thomas did the same.

How was he going to tell Thomas about the dead girl's arm? When should he tell him? Angela and Everett positioned themselves to one side and in front of the Cessna. They could see any conversation between him and Thomas, so he stayed quiet.

Thomas spent a moment examining the air map and checking the instruments. Out of the corner of his eye, Owen saw the man with the red hat, Luke, run up to Everett and whisper urgently in his ear. Everett glared at the plane, then gave some sort of order to Luke, who ran out of view. Did they know he'd found the girl's body?

"Clear prop!" Thomas pumped the throttle and turned the key, the engine spitting to life. Owen sat back in his seat, eyes straight ahead, and listened to the engine as Thomas adjusted the fuel mixture and checked the magnetos, turning first one off, then the other, then both back on for flight, Owen wishing he would hurry the hell up. Thomas finally pushed the throttle forward and the engine roared, the Cessna shuddered, and they began to roll down the dirt strip, vibrating, bouncing, jarring over small ruts until suddenly, liftoff, and the ride became smooth and even, the engine solid and throaty, clear air ahead of them, and Owen finally took a deep breath.

Thomas made a gentle turn to their left, flying back toward the creek, the dig site, and the old hangar, circling to gain altitude needed to fly over the plateau above the camp. They rose steadily as they went, Owen thinking how to explain what he'd found, hoping he'd done the right thing by waiting until they were in the air, bound for home base.

They leveled out about two miles past the Quonset hut, aiming for the broad Colorado River as they continued to climb beyond the canyon. A ribbon of dust rose to their right, a truck in motion along the road, soon to be well behind them. Ghost Creek faded from view as they neared the level of the plateau. They could see the bronze river beyond as it wound its way southward, on toward the Grand Canyon, on to the Gulf of California. Owen rubbed his hands on his pants and readied himself.

"Thomas," he spoke into the microphone on his headset.

"Yes?"

"I've got something to tell you, something I discovered down there while you were with the archeologist..."

"Yes?" Thomas checked his GPS and adjusted his heading.

Just then, a hollow thump jarred Thomas forward and he pushed the yoke in, then tugged and released it as he slumped back in his seat. Owen grabbed the yoke and his eyes swelled wide and he stared at Thomas' slackened face and began to scream his name, bobbing the plane's nose up, down, up, when another hollow thump jarred them and oil sprayed into the air and onto the right side of the windshield and he heard the motor cough, and cough again, and felt the Cessna lose its power, dropping in the air, descending toward the ground and he screamed again.

CHAPTER 18

Owen gripped the yoke and pulled it back, pushing the throttle full power. The nose of the small craft tilted upward but did not climb. The stall warning began to wail.

"Damn!" he swore, pushing the nose down again, watching the airspeed dial, keeping his glide about eighty miles per hour. Altitude was earned with engine power and he remembered that without it, a controlled glide was his best hope. Pulling up without power could put the plane into a uncontrolled stall and tail spin straight down to earth.

"If we were just a little higher, we could land on top of the plateau." Owen glanced at Thomas, hoping for a reply, but found none. A black slick crept across the right windowsill and sprayed off the edges.

What the hell was happening? Thomas, shot? The engine? His mind flashed to the tall man with the rifle.

The plane began a slow descent between blood-red canyon walls, their sides sharp as teeth.

"Oh, my god," Owen whispered, his eyes locked on the burly river below them. There was no place to land; their only choice was the river itself.

The canyon swallowed them whole.

Intense alarm threatened to whirl his thoughts out of control, but he tried to focus on first things first: keeping the wings level. He watched the horizon in front of him, fixing the plane in its limp, downward glide. He dropped the flaps a few degrees, because he'd heard that's what you do before a landing, and ruddered the Cessna down the middle of the coffee colored water. He angled the plane upward as it descended, reducing forward speed, pushing the limits of a stall, remembering what Thomas had showed him. Try as he might, he could not take his eyes off the river, rising ever more quickly to meet him.

The engine began to howl.

He strained to control the plane, turning the yoke left, then right, then left, struggling to keep the wings horizontal. Skimming inches above the gurgling torrent, the river filled his vision and he flared the Cessna one last time, tilting it radically upward, the water disappearing from view, the windshield now full of only sky, but at the same time dropping the plane as slowly as possible into the flowing runway. The stall warning whined its desperate pitch again and Owen took one last breath.

The Cessna's tail sliced the river an instant before its belly smacked the wet surface, skipping once like a flat stone, then torpedoing again down the turbid waterway. On the second impact, a metallic *smack!* echoed between the cliffs.

Thomas's earphones flew off of his head and clattered into the windshield, his hair and arms flailing like rags in a gale wind. Owen's arms strained against the woven shoulder straps, his chin levered tightly onto his chest, his breath choked off. Papers, maps, rags, and a small duffle bag flew past him from the rear.

A long wake rolled rapidly away from the fuselage. The left wing dipped into the river, spinning the plane counter-clockwise. Aluminum screeched as it tore apart and, in a moment, the metal shoulder separated from its riveted frame and twisted backwards on the strut like an elbow cracked and hinged in the wrong direction. The plane bobbed upwards as water showered the cockpit.

An icy chill soaked Owen's feet and crept up his pant legs. He tightened his hands into fists and blinked, water swirling like mocha at his ankles, miniature waves slapping against the cockpit wall.

The cabin seemed to spin, but he fought the urge to pass out. Carefully, he moved his head and looked around him. The windshield was twisted and cracked, but not shattered. His side window had popped out of its metal rim and the airplane rocked ominously in the unyielding current.

Thomas's hair covered his face, his arms and legs sprawled and limp. The river swirled and gurgled through a split in the cockpit floor.

"Hey!" Owen poked at Thomas's knee. "Hey!" he shouted again, grabbing the man's leg and shaking it. The motion made his head throb.

Owen tried to pull himself closer to Thomas, but his seat belt stopped him. He found the clasp and released it, then reached for Thomas's wrist. No pulse. He touched Thomas' neck then put his finger under Thomas's nose. No breath. There, on Thomas's other side, his chest was soaked with blood.

"Damn it!" Owen reeled away from him. Straightening his knees, Owen leaned toward his door and yanked on the handle. It wouldn't budge. He shifted his weight and pulled again.

The latch released, but the door did not move.

Water now was halfway up his calves and flowed around the outside of the plane at nearly the same level. Owen turned again toward Thomas and gently tilted his head back against the window. His lips were parted and slack, his face leaden, his eyes closed, thank god. Owen knew that he was gone.

Water bubbled from the floor, rising quickly to Owen's knees.

"Swim!" he shouted to himself and pushed against the door with all he had but it wouldn't budge and wouldn't budge until finally it began to crack slowly open. He jammed himself into the narrow space and pulled and twisted, slipping through. He gasped, then sunk under the river's surface, his fingers still holding the handle. The powerful current pulled him horizontally under the right wing and he released his grip, the water sweeping him away.

Eddies bounced him through the river like cottonwood seed in a summer storm. He spun downward, nearly to the riverbed, then upwards, just as quickly, spiraling to the surface and breaking free.

Green grass and high cliffs rose to his right. Owen swam furiously toward them, lungs heaving, nostrils stinging.

He paddled and scissor-kicked, arms and legs

aching, until finally his feet touched the stony bottom. His shoes slipped on the rocks, bruising his shins, and he rolled onto his hands and knees, hacking and shaking until he collapsed on a patch of grass on the sand, too weak to move.

CHAPTER 19

Relic ran along the old dirt track behind a low hill that hid the canyon and camps from view. The four-wheel path was an alternate route around the hill. He'd heard two rifle shots and seen smoke from the little aircraft before it made a drastic dip toward the river and out of his line of sight.

His pack bounced against his back and he slowed enough to tighten the shoulder straps.

Just ahead, the old track joined the smoother dirt road and turned sharply right, parallel with the river, following its flow to the south. He ran faster on the better road and his view opened along the wide meander.

A flash of light drew his eyes to a T-shaped, mirrored surface, bobbing in the deep current. He pushed himself to run faster, tripping on loose rock, catching himself, pushing again. The plane was shifting in the flow, its left wing crippled, bent awkwardly on the frame, disappearing under the water.

The road rose ahead of him and he powered higher until he reached the top and slowed his way down the other side. He skidded to a stop near the water's edge.

The plane appeared to be stuck on a rock, or maybe a sand bar beneath the surface, and it created crazy currents in the river flow, spinning circles, curlicue, and elongated vortexes that spun themselves out. Only its aluminum tail was left unsubmerged, a shark's fin parting the waters.

Relic looked around but saw no signs of life. If they were still inside the plane, they were already dead.

The current moved quickly and a swimmer could be carried downstream with little effort. He walked back to the road and moved down river, searching for places someone might have reached if they'd swum from the plane.

There. Something on a small beach to the side of the dirt road. Relic dropped his pack and ran to the body of a young man lying on the shore. Quickly, he folded the man's arms above his head and pushed hard against his ribs, expelling water, then air. He moved to the front of the man and pulled on his shoulders, opening his lungs like a bellows, then pushed again from behind, pulled, pushed from behind, pulled, and pushed until there was only air left the man's chest.

Relic rolled the young man over and listened closely to his ragged breath.

"Wake up!" Relic slapped the man's face. "Up!"

The man began to convulse, his stomach heaving, his shoulders buckling inward, and quickly Relic turned him over again and began to pound on his back. The man began to hack, vomiting water onto the ground, rasping, wheezing. In a moment, his coughing slowed and became more shallow and he shook his head and began to spit, pant for air, then spit some more. Relic laid the man on the ground, where he rested on his chest, shaking, his face turned toward the cliffs, his eyes closed tight. But he seemed past the worst of it.

Relic stood and went back for his pack, shouldered it, and returned. He sat for a moment as the man rested on the ground.

"What!" the man shouted and lifted himself in a push-up, river water dripping from his clothes. He pulled his legs under him, spun, and sat cross-legged. He moved his head back and forth slowly, wiped his face with his hands, and opened his eyes.

Relic slid close to the exhausted man and saw in his expression something bare, something stripped of the physical.

The man shook his head again. He seemed to be regaining his hearing and sight, his sense of self, his cheeks warming with the flow of blood.

Relic scooted away from him a bit. The man wore a brown shirt with a government patch on it, maybe some sort of park service uniform. A long, shallow wound on his side seeped blood.

"Thought maybe you'd already drowned." Relic's words seemed to wake the man from a dream. "Glad to see you made it back."

CHAPTER 20

"What?" Owen lifted his hands to his head and squeezed on his skull, trying to regain a sense of balance. The man across from him wore long, black hair in a ponytail tucked under an old green hat with some kind of insignia. He'd said something to him, but he couldn't tell what.

He coughed and cleared his throat. Exhaustion larded his muscles and his mind.

Crack! A shot came from up the road, on a high point, maybe three hundred yards away. At first, the sound was unreal, a theoretical bang in the soundless void, an interesting curiosity. Then Owen realized what he'd heard, how he'd been shot out of the air, and whatever was left of his adrenalin pumped into his brain in a tidal surge.

"Shit!" Owen jumped to his feet and ran toward

the cliff on the other side of the road.

"Wait!" the man with the ponytail leapt forward, chasing him across the road.

Crack! Gravel exploded behind Owen as his legs gained their rhythm, pumping against the dirt like pistons, propelling him into a field of boulders the size of cattle. He ducked below the first rock, crouching as he ran, stumbling his way down river, away from the sound of rifle fire.

He continued to run downriver until the boulders opened onto a meadow of sorts, filled with grasses, sage, and prickly pear cactus. Owen realized he was entering a new canyon, much smaller than the one the ruins were in. Dark sandstone cliffs rose sharply on the other side of the drainage. He kept moving, edging to the west, he thought, working his way up the gorge but staying among the rocks, avoiding open ground. He slowed to a fast walk and developed a regular pace, glancing behind him from time to time, scouting ahead as the canyon wound its crooked path, sheer, burnt-red walls rising and narrowing as he went. Just where the hell was he?

The last of his adrenalin seemed to fade, and fatigue weighed on him like a wet wool jacket. His steps became shorter and shorter and he took more frequent breaks to catch his breath and look around.

He'd heard no more shots since the first two, but there was no telling whether the rifleman was following him or not. And who was this guy with the ponytail?

Around a jumble of boulders, an arroyo spread before him, and he decided to take that route. Though more open, the going would be easier and faster. The sandy bottom was far better to walk on and he soon found himself winding around another sharp bend in the canyon. His energy waning, he found a flat rock at the edge of the drainage and sat in some shade.

He leaned forward and placed his head in his hands, catching his breath, trying to relax.

Thomas. Thomas was dead. He remembered the man's face, slack, empty, gone, then panic when he'd grabbed the yoke of the plane, in control but out of control, aiming toward the only option he had: a roaring, bubbling river. He sobbed.

What the hell was he going to do now? There was no telling how long this canyon was, or where it topped off onto the plateau, or whether he could climb to the plateau at all. Water. He had no water to drink, nothing with him but…his phone. He reached hurriedly onto his belt and pulled the phone from its case. River water dripped from the hand-sized screen and he shook it and laid it on the rock to dry. Oh, God, please let it work. If he could get to a high spot…

The sound of boots scraping against the sand reached his ears and he stiffened. Shit. He had to escape back to the road along the river, hike out for help if he had to. He could ambush the bastard… but with what?

The sound suddenly stopped. A dense silence filled the small canyon like thickened air, his sense of hearing muted and distorted under it all, the tiny bleep of bird calls like early warnings for a booming rifle he expected at any moment. He dared not move.

"Hey," a deep voice echoed against the cliff. "I'm not armed. I'm coming on up to where you are, but don't shoot, OK?"

He thinks I'm armed, Owen thought, straining to hear. No movement yet.

"Hey, we're both running from the same guy. A man with a rifle, remember? He shot down your plane and tried to kill us back there, along the road."

Owen did not need a reminder.

"I helped you, flushed the water from your lungs, remember? My name's Relic."

"Relic?"

"I've gotta come on up, so just don't shoot me, OK?"

Boots struck the ground in even steps and

the man with the ponytail emerged into the light, hands raised, stepping slowly across the flats of the arroyo, looking directly at Owen. How did he know where Owen was?

"Take off your pack." Owen reached behind him, hoping the man would think he had a pistol under his belt.

Relic lowered his pack to the ground and raised his arms into the air.

"Move over here." Owen pointed about twenty feet away. Relic nodded and walked closer.

"Here OK?"

"Yes. Sit there."

"Now what?"

"Who are you and what are you doing here?"

Relic sat on a low rock, his knees higher than his waist, and lowered his arms onto his legs, keeping his hands open and visible.

"I'm out here on a hike, exploring around the Ghost House ruins, when I see some kind of archeologic dig down by the stream." He glanced at the ground. "I see this guy, a tall drink of water with a rifle on his shoulder and he's walking around like some sort of security, like he's on patrol. And he likes to target practice with that thirty-ought-six of his and he's pretty good too. So I keep my distance."

"You're with that crew, the owner's representatives, aren't you?"

"Owners? No, I don't know who they are. I've seen their camp, separate from the younger folks doing the dig."

"Students." Owen shook his head, regretting his words. He should be running an interrogation. Sharing information with a suspect was not proper procedure.

"Students. That might explain it."

"Explain what?"

"They work under a woman's supervision in the mornings, when it's cooler, and then meet under a canopy after lunch. The woman always seems to be lecturing them, and I guess she is."

"You want me to believe you're just some hiker who happened to come by?"

"That's pretty much it."

"Bullshit."

"No shit."

"What else is going on over there?"

"Hell if I know. Weird stuff."

"Like what?"

Relic leaned to his left, searching for a better view of Owen's arm, still tucked behind him, still pretending to grip a pistol. It was pathetic, Owen knew, but he was scared out of his mind and bravado seemed to be his only option. He turned and reached for a baseball-sized rock and held it up, as if to throw it at Relic.

Relic looked back at Owen's face. "OK. But let me ask you this – did you see me down there? Was I any part of that group?"

Owen knew the answer was "no" but clamped his lips tight against the urge to say it.

"The only thing I've done so far is save your ass. It'd be respectful of you to point that rock somewhere else, you know."

With these words, Owen's threat seemed all the more ridiculous, but he doubled down. "No chance."

"So, what's our situation, here, buddy?"

"As a Park Service officer, you're my prisoner."

"I see."

CHAPTER 21

"Look, we really don't have time for this." Relic stood and stretched.

"Sit back down." Owen raised the stone.

Relic put his boot on a rock, looked sideways at Owen, and grinned. "There's some maniac with a rifle following us and he can't be too far behind. If you want a way out of this little canyon and water to drink, you'd best follow me."

Owen thought about the man who'd shot at them, who'd killed Thomas.

"But if you're going to attack me, you'd best kill me quickly. After that, the rifleman will know exactly where you are and he'll pick you off like a tick on deer hide."

Owen looked at the rock in his hand. Shit.

Relic walked to his pack and shouldered it.

"It's OK, officer. I'm still your prisoner, if that's what you want. But your prisoner knows a way out of this mess, so I'd suggest you follow me." Relic turned and began to walk further up the arroyo, his pace steady and unhurried.

Shit. Owen dropped the stone and picked up his phone, already drying in the heat. He shook excess water from the holder and replaced the phone into it. His clothes were still mostly wet from the river, drying from the edges in, and he'd begun to cool in the shade. Who the hell does this guy think he is? He hurried to catch up, warming under the afternoon sun.

Relic kept a steady pace as they rounded another bend in the canyon, its high walls tightening as they ascended. They walked for nearly an hour, twisting with the dry creek bed until the canyon opened a bit, a stale pool of water at the head of the drainage. Owen stopped to catch his breath.

An alcove sixty feet high rose above the little pond, layers of scarlet and gray sandstone sculpted into a smooth, curving bowl turned nearly upside-down, a notch in the middle where the water fell from the top when it rained. Delicate, fern-like plants clung to wet cracks along the back of the bowl, gleaming pea-green leaves quaking against the dark stone. Cliffs towered even higher than the dry waterfall, climbing into the afternoon sky, shrinking the blue to a narrow triangle above their heads. Quiet wrapped around them like a cool blanket in the shade. A lone crow hovered higher up the canyon then banked away.

Wait, Owen thought. There's no way out of here. They were caught in a box canyon, just like he was afraid of. Where the hell has this guy brought them? What's he really up to?

He looked around. And where the hell is he?

CHAPTER 22

"Hey!" Relic stepped from behind a chunk of fallen cliff and waved him over.

"What? What are you doing?" He walked toward Relic.

"Over here. A way up."

Owen moved to the side of the pool and looked beyond Relic, searching for the way. He went cautiously closer.

"We climb these two rocks here," Relic pointed toward the face of the cliff, "then go up by rope."

"Rope?"

"Right. It's a bit tricky but a good route."

Shit. It looked impossible. "How did that get here?" He pointed to a faded rope that looked twenty years old.

"If you gotta know, it's mine. I got four or

five of 'em in this back-country, at spots it's tough to climb up."

"Yours?" This guy is no casual hiker.

"You want to go first, or me?" Relic tugged on his goatee and smiled. The guy wasn't even breathing hard, wasn't even tired. He even seemed to be having fun.

"You first," Owen pointed to the rope.

Relic turned and scrambled up the rocks that rested on the floor of the canyon, then lifted himself on a ledge along the cliff and reached for the rope. From there, he placed his feet against the wall and moved slowly upward, hand over hand on the rope, his toes finding purchase where he could, his legs helping as he went until he reached the top. He scrambled on hands and knees above the dry waterfall, a good seventy feet above Owen and the pond. Relic stood, removed his pack, and rested it on the ground. He turned and squatted by the rope at the very edge of the cliff.

Owen knew the guy could leave him down here, if he wanted. What was he really up to?

Relic motioned Owen to come up.

Or, Owen thought, he could cut the rope when Owen was half way up. Assuming it didn't break first. But then, what choice did he have?

Owen touched his phone holder, made sure it

was snapped shut, patted his stomach, and stared at the top of the cliff. He walked to the first rock, climbed up, then stepped onto the next and hugged the sandstone face. Relic wiggled the rope above Owen's head, just within reach.

He grabbed the rope with both hands and lifted himself until his left arm was fully bent at the elbow, then slid his right higher and held tight. He churned his feet like he would bicycle pedals, scratching desperately for some kind of foothold on the rock. His right foot found a thin grip for a moment but slipped off, pulling him down to where he began, both of his arms straight again on the rope.

"Shit." He hung there, catching his breath. "I can't do this."

"You almost had it. Get that first foothold and stand up on it, then hand to hand."

Owen searched the slick rock face for that tiny hold and pulled himself up again, aiming his foot for the grip. Sweat rolled down his temple and arms, and he heaved and struggled and finally found some purchase on the rock. Muscles shaking, he straightened his right leg, all of his weight on that knee, and slid his hands up the rope as he went.

Clack! The sound of rock on rock echoed up the narrow canyon.

CHAPTER 23

Owen focused intently on the smooth stone, inches from his face, and began to pull himself higher up, hand over hand, chin-up after chin-up, his legs useless under him now, hanging, scraping noisily against the unyielding cliff, his breathing uneven and desperate, his shoulders shaking under the strain. The cliff beveled away from him as he neared the top and, when he raised his left arm for the rope one more time, Relic grasped it below Owen's wrist and leaned backward, pulling Owen the last three feet onto the top and onto his stomach. Owen's face slid into fine gravel on the ground but the discomfort meant nothing to him now, his left leg cramped in pain, his arms liquid with exhaustion, air rasping in and out of his lungs on its own volition.

"I have you ass-wipes now." Luke's voice echoed in the alcove, sharp and cold.

Owen's breath slowly came back to him, and he rolled over and away from the ledge. He massaged the cramp in his calf as Relic pulled the rope up behind them and tied it to a bush. Relic held his finger to his lips and offered Owen his hand.

He pulled his legs under himself and rose with Relic's help. His knees buckled for a moment then he caught himself and stood up again. They walked slowly away from the exposed ledge and along a wide, level basin of solid rock, each step closer to safety. The canyon opened a bit here, the cliffs receding from the dry creek bed, a whole other world of distant ridges, sloping grasslands, juniper and saltbush. Relic hastened their pace for another three hundred yards, now fully out of sight from anyone in the alcove. He pulled them to a sandy spot in the shade of the high cliff and sat.

Owen rested his back against a stone and wished never to move again, no matter what. His left leg still ached from the cramp, his lips felt like chipped wood, his arms hot with sunburn, his head pounding like a jackhammer.

"Here," Relic offered.

Owen squinted at the offered bottle, the lid already removed. He took hold of it gingerly, with both hands, so as not to drop it, and poured a swallow down his throat. Nothing had ever tasted so healthy, so nurturing. He took another swallow, and then another, drinking until his stomach tugged under the weight of it all. He stopped and handed the water back to Relic, who finished the last of it.

Owen closed his eyes and sucked in the sweet desert air. He imagined his body absorbing fresh water into his blood, his tear ducts, his cracked lips, expanding, reviving like a living sponge. Just when he knew he never wanted to move again, he heard Relic clear his throat.

"Daylight's burning." Relic was standing, adjusting his pack.

CHAPTER 24

She wiped the sweat from her eyes with the bottom of her T-shirt and stepped back from the sifter. The aluminum contraption stood waist-high and held a four-wheeled tray on a track that let her slide it back and forth. Others brought her raw dirt, one bucket at a time, and she dropped it onto the screen at the bottom of a wide drawer. Smaller pieces fell to another bucket below when she rolled it, and she could examine larger chunks on the screen for pottery shards, arrowheads, needles, pieces of decorative shell. She'd found a small spindle whorl yesterday, the highlight of her work so far. The disk-shaped stone had a hole in the center that lets it fit partway down a spindle-stick. The weight of the whorl helps gather and spin cotton or plant fibers into thread. Someone had rested in the grass by the lazy creek and spun thread for maybe a shirt, a doll, or a pouch, eight hundred years ago.

Suzy looked out across the open ground to the trees along Ghost Creek, their shiny leaves twitching in the afternoon breeze. A nasty storm had blown through the canyon the night before, dumping heavy rain for over ten minutes before it rolled itself upriver. Parched plants and sandy ground soaked up the cool relief, but by this afternoon the sun was sucking the moisture back out, the earth sweating her musky scents into the desert air.

Above the thin stream rose a bank of cliffs, and perched atop was a row of ancient masonry, ruins of what was once a thriving Pueblo community. She tossed her baseball cap on the ground and tucked her dark hair behind her ears.

Angela had helped the students locate the approved dig area with a GPS device. They'd leveled the ground by hand and established grids or quads tied to GPS locator numbers and an altimeter. Angela had assigned each grid to two or more students, who rotated periodically with those who worked the sifter. The students dug with trowels, pushing dirt and rock to the side as they went, then collecting that for screening. Anything found along the way was photographed and recorded in situ, then carefully removed.

Suzy needed three laboratory credits and this course on field archeology fit the bill. The class consisted of six hours a day, including moderate work on the site plus instruction time, for about eighteen days, including travel time to and from the campus. She found the work intriguing and the canyon itself something of a life-sized movie by National Geographic, an alternate reality, stunning in its scope and even a bit confusing in its depth. She wondered what it would be like to see it from the air.

"More dirt?" Bruce's voice broke into her thoughts.

"Sure," she pointed to the empty tray.

"Same quadrangle as the last one."

She logged it as the second bucket from that spot today.

"You look hot." He poured the loose dirt across the open screen and stepped back. "How are your hands?"

"My hands?" she looked at them.

He moved quickly to her and reached for her fingers. "Everyone's hands are dry and cracking with this work."

His hand touched hers and she pulled away. "I'm OK."

"Yeah, yours still look good." His eyes examined her hands, and then the rest of her, from under his brow.

"Right." She moved back to the sifter, her lips tight.

"Angela says meet back at the lecture tent in twenty." Bruce turned slowly and walked away. "See you there!"

Her stomach clenched for a moment and she focused again on the dirt on the screen. A little creepy, she thought as he walked away. A little too forward, too. But soon enough she found her rhythm again, moving the drawer forward, then back, forward, then back, as dust and small pieces of dirt dropped below. She sifted through all of the loose dirt Bruce had brought her from the pit, not a very full bucket this time. Nothing of interest.

She covered the sifter with the small tarp Angela had brought for that purpose and anchored the bottom with rocks. She tucked the small log book under her arm. Over a small rise, she could see that the other students had already stopped for the day, making their way toward a large canopy and camp chairs set up for daily de-briefings and short lectures from Angela. So far, they'd found some interesting artifacts – two chert knives, pottery shards, small animal bones, a fire pit, and her spindle whorl. The ruins across the creek were on federal land, and they'd need a permit to dig there. The land here was private, all the way to the edge of the water.

She brushed the dirt from her pants and began the half-mile walk to the makeshift lecture hall. She hadn't met most of the other students before this class, but she got along well with them. Tonight they'd planned a party, behind Angela's back. Angela had been a bit of a hard-ass earlier, but she wasn't unfair. Suzy assisted her when she could, not just as a student aide, but because it let her ask more personal questions, like why Angela liked teaching at the college, what she liked about archeology, careers in the field, that sort of thing. She got to tag along when Angela gave the Park Service pilot a quick tour.

Suzy tugged at the band that kept her long hair together and realized she'd forgotten her hat. She took the log book in her hand, turned and trotted back down the light trail to the sifter and searched for her blue Broncos cap. When she found it, she tugged it on and flapped her ponytail through the opening in back. She turned to run back toward the student camp and noticed two men carrying boxes to the open dig. The owner's representatives. The fast talker was Everett, she remembered, and the big cowboy was Johnson. What were they doing? The students had all been told these men would observe the site and check the records that Angela created each day about what they'd found. It made sense that they were watching out for the land-owner, but…why were they carrying cardboard boxes to the site? What was in them?

She crept behind a tall batch of sage brush and watched. Everett, the man she thought of as a salesman, leaned over a box, and she could see a camera hanging from his neck. Johnson removed something from one of the containers and seemed to place it into the pit, just below the surface of the surrounding area. Why were they messing with the site? Weren't they taint-ing it? Blades of grass danced in the hot breeze and blocked her view.

She turned back toward camp and moved away as quickly and quietly as she could, tucking the log book back under her arm.

CHAPTER 25

Owen leaned forward and tried to get his exhausted legs underneath him.

"I've got a camp just a bit further up canyon, water, and some supplies. Not far," Relic pointed.

Owen rose slowly, his knees rubbery, his balance tenuous. He looked across the open field, where islands of sage and Mormon tea dotted the grassy plain. Humps of pinkish sandstone, striped with bands of gray, rested like giants in the distant, snoring under the desert sun. He'd never seen so many rocks or so many kinds and shapes of rocks – ramparts baked blood-red in the desert kiln; tall, lonely spires; wide, muscled towers; massive scoops of sodden sand dropped and dried into place. Was he really on planet earth?

Relic watched him for a moment and turned his eyes across the canyon too. "Leaves you a little breathless, doesn't it?"

Owen nodded.

"Can you make it? Go a little further?"

"Yeah." He put one foot forward, then the other, and Relic led the way along the bottom of a cliff, taking it slowly.

Owen moved his tired feet across the ground and shuffled around loose stones and cacti, eyes downcast, concentrating on the effort. After a while, he and Relic turned to their right and entered cooling shadows and an overhang of rock above level, sandy ground. Relic entered a hidden grotto, walked to the back and removed his pack. Owen followed mindlessly until he reached Relic and looked up.

"Sit where you like. Time for some rest." Relic went to a large, white bucket and dipped his water bottle into it. "Rain water," he said. "Seriously – sit and rest."

Owen was afraid he'd never get up again, but he bent his knees and lowered himself quickly into the dirt. The overhang curved gently from the ground until it formed an unbroken wall and extended above them. He felt the jab of his phone holder and he pulled it out. It appeared to be dry, so he turned it on and let it run through its routine.

Owen sensed Relic watching him. "I'm checking my phone." He shifted his feet to a more comfortable position. "In case I can call or email for help." He kept his eyes on the flat rectangle and began to move his fingers across the screen.

Relic watched him.

"I'll check for coverage. And any emails that might have come through when Thomas, the pilot, and I were flying."

"No phone service here."

"Maybe I can drop a pin or send a screenshot or some other message for help, but I can't seem to find anything. Can't get google to work, can't see any new tweets." He moved his fingers across the screen again and again, tapping hastily. "I don't expect 4G but there must be some kind of coverage..." Agitated, he swiped the phone with increasing fervor.

"Humpf." Relic crossed his arms.

"Hell, man, haven't you seen a smartphone before?" Owen glanced up in frustration.

"Sure I have. You tweet and pin and play games on a screen. It distracts you from reality."

"What? No, man, it connects you with reality."

Relic shook his head. "You're talking gibberish."

"Holy eff," Owen took a breath and looked up at

Relic. "How long have you been out here, in the middle of nowhere?"

"No, my friend. We're at the center of the universe." Relic pointed outside their little alcove, at the distant cliffs.

"How do you figure that?"

"When the universe is infinite, well then, anywhere you are, you are in the middle of it."

Owen lowered the phone to the ground, leaned against the cool sandstone, and closed his eyes. It was Relic's turn for gibberish. But the truth was, he'd never been to a place like this.

Relic moved toward the back of the overhang and sat down. "We need to have a talk later."

Owen opened an eye and squinted.

Relic sucked a long drink and wiped the dripping water from his goatee. "Prisoner to captor, I mean," he grinned.

Owen closed his eye again and groaned.

CHAPTER 26

Damn it all. Luke searched the rocks above the little alcove but could not see anyone.

Where the hell did they go? He adjusted his ammunition sling and pulled his arm through the shoulder strap on the rifle. He trotted from one side of the drainage to the other, peering for a second time behind rocks, even those too small to hide anyone, checking again and again for any sign of the two men. Somehow, they'd gotten above him and escaped. He could see no way to follow them up the slick, rock walls. Finally exhausted, he turned and walked back down the winding arroyo, stopping now and then to peer above him for any movement, any sign of his targets he might have missed.

After nearly an hour, Luke could hear water powering through its channel, waves lapping on rocks along the shore. The canyon opened again here and the dirt road formed a straight line next to the wide, meandering river. Upstream, he could see the shiny tail of the drowned Cessna, its rudder bent tightly against the flow.

He adjusted the Winchester on his shoulder and walked along the road toward his truck and the camp. The location of the plane, he figured, was good news and bad news. Most of it was hidden. From the air, the tail might not even be noticed – it probably appeared in the river like a finger of wet rock, a thread-like glare on the water. But from the ground, the tail was unmistakably out of place. A slice of silver as wide as a door rose four feet from the surface, forcing the tense current to part around it, sending little water tornados swirling down the river. Anyone using the road along this spot would understand it was part of an airplane. He'd counted on downing the plane on the ground, where he could cover it with canvas tarps, rocks, and dirt. Out there, in the water, he could do nothing to hide it.

He continued along a bend in the two-track road, the smell of the river reminding him how thirsty he'd become. The sight of his long-bed truck, parked where he'd taken his shots at the plane, was a welcome relief.

Luke turned the pickup around and drove back carefully over the rutted road. Eventually, he rumbled past the big turn by the hill and could see the dig site and camp about a mile away. Cold, fresh water and icy beer awaited him. He could see that the students were gathering under their canopy, done digging in the hot sun until tomorrow. Everett and Johnson were walking back from the site, carrying boxes to the central tent. Luke stopped the truck nearby and strode into the shade near the Quonset hut. He found a camp chair by the large cooler, slid the rifle from his shoulder, and sat down.

"What happened?" Everett sat beside him.

Luke pulled out a bottle of water, opened it, and poured it down his throat. When he could drink no more, he wiped his mouth with the back of his hand and took several deep breaths.

"Hot out there, I know." Everett reached into the cooler for a beer. Johnson appeared at the entrance to the big tent where they worked and folded his arms.

"So, what's the deal?" Everett leaned forward and clamped his hands around the cold can.

"Good news is, they didn't fly away and the plane is down." Luke dropped the empty water bottle to the ground. He laid the Winchester across his lap, pulled a rag from his pants, and began to clean dust off the wooden stock.

Everett sat up straight, his eyes tightly on Luke's,

his question clear.

"Get me a beer, would you?" Luke glanced at Johnson.

"Get it yourself."

"What else happened?" Everett leaned forward, annoyance in his voice. He handed his beer to Luke and pulled another one from the cooler.

Luke stopped cleaning the rifle and sat back into his chair. "I knew they had to be taken out. If I hadn't, they'd be talking to the feds right now. I didn't have a chance to shoot until they'd started to leave the area, out over the little hill by the road."

"And?"

"So, I shot 'em out of the sky, I did, right out of the sky." He grinned at Everett, then at Johnson.

"You said 'good news,' Luke, like there might be some bad news too." Everett lowered his brow.

"Mostly good, some not so much." Luke popped the beer and took a swig of it. "Plane went down in the river, and it's almost all covered up, but the tail is sticking out and 'cause it's in the river, we can't cover it up."

"Shit." Johnson turned and paced away from the tent, hand on his forehead.

"How much is sticking out? Can you see it?" Everett squeezed his beer can.

"The whole tail. You probably can't see it from the air but sure as hell can from the road."

"OK." Everett looked over at Johnson for a moment. "What else?"

"The pilot's dead, but the Park Service kid got away from me."

"What?" Johnson moved closer to them.

"How?" Everett spread his hands.

"I don't know how, but one of them, the kid, the one we're thinking found the bodies – he was along the river when I got there. But there was another guy, a hiker I guess, there with him. They took off up a little canyon near the road and I chased them way up there, to a box canyon, but somehow they'd gotten on the next layer up, you know, so they could keep going up. I looked all over and still I don't know how they did it. I couldn't find any way up to that next level."

"Gawdammit, Luke, you were supposed to take care of this!" Everett stood from his chair.

"You've really screwed this up," Johnson clenched his hands into fists and took a step toward Luke.

Luke slid a shell into the Winchester on his lap and aimed it casually at Johnson.

"Knock it off!" Everett paced between them. "We've all got to figure this out…so let's take a deep breath. Me included," he pointed to himself.

Johnson looked at Everett, his lips tight.

Luke turned slowly to Everett. "What do you want us to do now?"

"We're going to have to shut down, but it's OK. We've got some time to break camp and move out."

"There's two guys loose out there, ready to turn us in to the local sheriff or the FBI…" Johnson pointed south, toward where the plane had gone down.

"Yeah, but they've got no water, no food, no phone service," Everett rubbed his forehead. "They're on foot. It's thirty-plus miles to the highway. We've got wheels. We finished a big batch today and are getting down on our supplies anyway."

Johnson folded his arms across his chest again and watched as Everett moved about, thinking it through.

Luke aimed his rifle at the ground, a gesture of cooperation.

"We can do this. It's Friday evening now. We finish this batch and Johnson, you take it out tomorrow. Come back for a final load and we're all out of here before nightfall on Sunday, Monday at the latest."

"Won't somebody notice that the Park Service kid and the pilot are missing?"

"If no one comes looking by tomorrow morning,

they won't come until Tuesday, after the three day week-end. We can't possibly get everything ready and out of here tonight anyway and I'm not leaving without these last two loads, they're worth way too much cash. So if they show up tomorrow we hunker down, play dumb, bluff a little. Maybe bury the ledgers and the cash box, temporarily. And if no one shows by noon tomorrow, we're home free 'till Tuesday and we'll be on the road in plenty of time before then."

"What about the students?" Johnson nodded toward their camp.

"Nothing. We leave them here. Tell them the owner scheduled us to come back to her place for a report. We tell them we'll be back…"

"They'll have no ride out of the canyons," Johnson said.

"So? They'll all walk out or people looking for the pilot will take them out. By then, we'll be scattered in all different directions."

"I don't like leaving witnesses." Luke rubbed the stock on his rifle.

"Shit, Luke," Johnson swung his arms upward, "they haven't seen anything incriminating and besides… you can't just shoot a whole camp full of college kids."

"Use your head now, Luke." Everett's voice was

firm but soothing.

"If you have one," Johnson whispered.

CHAPTER 27

Suzy sat in the shade of a thick box elder near Ghost Creek, reviewing her notes and thinking about what they'd learned so far about archeological field work. The overriding principle was that finds be meticulously recorded for location, depth below the surface, relationship with other artifacts found in the vicinity, cultural context. A pre-history puzzle, it was; the archeologist reconstructing ancient technologies, lifestyles, patterns of migration, and more, then testing theories against the evidence.

After the daily mini-lecture, Angela had gone to the tents of the owner's representatives and stayed most of the evening again, probably preparing the field notes and records. She seemed to be spending more and more time there, and less with the students, not that Suzy blamed her. Did Angela know what Everett, Luke, and

Johnson were doing with cardboard boxes at the dig site each day, after the students left?

She closed her notebook. Her computer was of little use here, out beyond the internet, with limited opportunities to recharge the battery, so she'd abandoned it altogether for this class. It was weird to return to hand-written notes, scratched out errors, pages that tore and crinkled when they got wet. It made everything slower, messier, but it helped her absorb the material too, tie it all together.

There was no shade under the nearby canopy now, the angled sun stretching shadows across the meadow, merging them with the scattered lines of student tents. Dusk reached across the field, blending murkiness into night.

To the west, the sun exploded sideways atop the high canyon rim, smearing light across the sky and making her blink. In a few moments, the ball of fire fell below the horizon and the cliff became backlit in rouge and wine, spokes of faded, translucent sky jetting into space. She watched until the sun became a muted glow, a star spinning away from their little world at eight hundred miles per hour.

The sharp clank of enameled plates reached her ears and turned her attention back to camp. As the

other student aide, it was Victor's turn to clean up
after the meal.

The students had finished supper some time ago,
but now she heard them gathering food from their storage canisters and, no doubt, liquor from their private
supplies. There would be another party tonight. The
flicker of a campfire reached her eyes from the distance,
small as the flame on a cigarette lighter. Raucous voices
carried on the breeze, the sound of exclamations and
laughter puncturing the quiet.

A jaundiced shimmer inside the big tents silhou-
etted where Everett, Luke, and Johnson stayed. She
resolved to find Angela and ask what those men were
doing at the dig site each day, after the students were
gone, or to eavesdrop, if she could, to figure it out.
She dusted off her pants and began moving toward the
glowing tents.

CHAPTER 28

Flames snapped and whispered eagerly in the concave shelter, waking Owen. The tiny fire was ringed with bowl-sized rocks.

"Hungry?" Relic shoved the last of something into his mouth and chewed it slowly.

Where the hell was he? At first, Owen's muscles refused to move, but then he rolled stiffly onto his right side and lifted himself into a sitting position. The effort made him heave a deep breath and he crossed his legs under him and rested. Oh, yeah, he remembered. He was in the middle of nowhere.

"Water?" He heard his own voice croak.

Relic handed him a plastic bottle and Owen poured it down his throat in long, deep swallows. When he could drink no more, he set the bottle next to Relic and stared at the throbbing blaze.

"Here," Relic leaned forward and handed Owen a bag of beef jerky. "You've been asleep for a while. You need to eat something." Relic sat back and began chewing on a new piece of jerky, his goatee exaggerated in the firelight shadows, an ape-man masticating on mammoth meat.

Owen popped some of the dried beef into his mouth. His dormant taste buds sprang to life, sweet Tennessee barbeque mixing with the sharp taste of salt, the feel of tender meat squishing under his molars, and he became his own cave dwelling carnivore.

"Have a bit of homemade gin, if you like." Relic offered him a pint-sized plastic flask, the lid hanging from its neck like a dog tag.

Owen swallowed his jerky and reached for the gin. He took a breath, then swung his head back and poured the drink down his throat, its icy burn making him cough. He held the container for a moment.

"It's gin?"

"Some say homemade gin, some say moonshine." Relic flashed a smile.

Owen took another swallow then motioned for more water.

Relic chuckled and handed him the bottle.

"Wow." Owen took a few measured drinks, washing the moonshine past his searing tongue.

Relic poured a shot of gin down this throat and handed it back to Owen again, who took another swallow, followed quickly with more water. Owen took another bite of jerky, and he chewed more slowly on it this time, feeling the warmth of the gin, the filling of his stomach, breathing the scent of burning wood and cool night air. His muscles loosened with the liquor and relaxed in the heat from the fire. He shifted in the sand to a more comfortable position.

Owen peered beyond their shallow overhang. Stars scattered haphazardly across the night sky, some clustered, some all alone, floating across the deep expanse like a migration of fireflies caught in the moment. And here he was, as Relic put it, in the center of the universe, the middle of everywhere.

He suddenly remembered his smart phone and considered whether to try again to get it to work. Then he wondered just what Relic had wanted to talk to him about.

CHAPTER 29

Everett set two lanterns on the ground inside the large tent and sat in a camp chair toward the back. Six boxes lined up neatly on the folding tables in the middle, his work done for the evening. He took a deep breath and thought about getting a cold beer from the cooler.

Footsteps sounded outside the tent and Johnson pushed back the flap and peered through. Everett waved him inside.

Johnson's shadow rose above him onto the roof of the tent, elongated by the low-sitting lights. He lifted a chair from the ground, unfolded it, and sat a couple of feet from Everett.

"How goes it?" Everett crossed his feet and leaned forward.

"Those college kids are having a party tonight."

"Ah, let 'em, they gotta blow off some steam. It'll

keep 'em occupied."

"Drunk is what you mean, Everett. The party'll keep 'em drunk. They'll be bumping and humping each other all night long."

Everett smiled. "Sure, like you've never been young and drunk…"

Johnson took his cowboy hat off and rubbed his crew-cut hair. "Well…"

"Otherwise, things going OK?"

"Yeah, I think so. How about on your end?"

"Well…" Everett grasped one hand with the other.

"What?"

"Honestly, it's Luke…"

"What about him?" Johnson put his hat back on and the light bounced in strange ways across his face.

"Look, can we talk about this confidentially, just the two of us?"

"Sure."

"I've been thinking and worrying about this. Here's the deal." He leaned farther forward. "Luke has screwed up at least three big ways since we got here. First," he raised a finger, "he didn't bury those delinquents deep enough. The storm came through that night, with some serious rain, and by morning, the

damn girl's arm is sticking up in the air like a signpost."
He looked at Johnson.

"Second," he raised another finger, "he was supposed to kill that pilot and the Park Service guy, to clean
up his first mistake. He shot 'em out of the sky, but the
park guy lives. Hell, Johnson, Luke's got the rifle and
the full advantage…"

Johnson looked to the ground and nodded.

"Third," Everett raised another finger, "the Park
Service guy meets up with some hiker guy, we guess,
and Luke lets both of them get away clean. Now, we
have to move out sooner than we planned, in case those
two make it back to the sheriff."

Johnson looked up at Everett.

"Hell, man, we're working on borrowed time
right now." Everett shook his head and rubbed his
hands together.

"So, we should move along faster, huh?"
Johnson said.

Good god, Everett thought, "move along faster"?
If Johnson and Luke had brains that moved along at all,
it would be a miracle. But two mindless twits together
might just cancel each other out…and provide some
opportunities.

Everett shifted in his chair. "Before that, we have

to decide what to do with Luke."

Johnson sat up, his hands on his knees.

"He's gone from shooting at scarecrows and airplanes to shooting those delinquents. He did us a favor, there, but I think the guy is turning into a real, cold-blooded killer."

Johnson sat in silence, his expression unreadable. "What are you suggesting?"

"I'm not suggesting anything anymore. I'm saying you and I have to eliminate Luke before he screws up again, like shooting co-eds for target practice. You heard him suggest it when we talked earlier..."

"That's true," Johnson nodded.

"Nobody will miss those two delinquents, but if Luke starts shooting college kids, there'll be no hiding that and we are all going to the electric chair. We have to deal with Luke before that happens."

Johnson pushed his hat tightly against his head. "I get it."

"And before he eliminates us…"

"Shit."

"There's an upside, though…" Everett's grin exaggerated under the harsh lantern. "If you'll take out Luke, you can have his share of the split, all of it."

Johnson sat up straighter.

"Hey, it's worth it to me, man," Everett spread his hands. "You do the task, you ought to have a hundred percent of his share. We'll both be better off."

CHAPTER 30

Owen pulled his phone from its holder and searched again in vain for an internet connection. He stopped for a moment and glanced up. Relic just sat there, some kind of prehistoric man, his unshaven face glowing in the small fire, his eyes alive, strands of unruly hair like black wires reaching out, connecting with the dark of outer space. Not the least bit concerned with the electrical portal to the world that Owen held in his hands, not a clue about how important it all was.

Relic cleared his throat. "It's got a hold on you, friend, and it's not making you a better man. Those lights, they're addicting for a reason."

"Bullshit."

"No shit."

"I am not 'addicted,' as you say, to anything." His eyes returned to the screen.

"Sure as shit, that's it. You're hooked."

"No, I'm not." He began moving his fingers across the screen again. "Nothing but old messages and spam in the inbox..."

"Spam's a piece of meat in a can."

"Damn connection. Nothing at all way out here."

"Everything is out here," Relic reached for the phone and slipped it gently from Owen's fingers.

"Hey!" Owen reached toward Relic, who leaned away from him.

Relic held the phone over his head. "Let it go for a while. We need to talk about what happened."

"Give that back to me." Owen pushed himself onto his knees and reached closer to Relic.

Relic scooted farther away.

Owen stood and pointed at Relic. "Give me back my phone right now, or..."

"Just take a breath, will you?"

Owen pulled a lit branch from the fire and moved it toward Relic.

"You're in worse shape than I thought."

"It's mine, just give it back."

"You're starting to sound like a third grader..."

Owen's face flushed. "Damn it," he raised the flaming stick at Relic and held out his other hand.

"Give it to me."

"Please?" Relic smiled.

"Please…"

Relic reached over the small fire and handed the phone across. Owen's fingers grasped the thin device, but as he moved for a tighter hold, the phone slid from his hand and dropped straight down into the flames, sending sparks into the night air.

"Shit, shit, shit," Owen tried twice to reach into the heat with his free hand, but he was driven back each time. He lowered the stick he'd pointed at Relic and began poking the flames with it, shifting the hot coals, trying desperately to slide the phone out. Finally, the blackened phone slid over the stones in the fire ring and out onto the dust, smoldering.

Owen sat on the ground, staring at the crackling device. He tossed the stick into the fire, closed his eyes, and sighed.

"Now that looks like spam to me," Relic leaned forward for a better view. "Just right, too. A little crisp around the edges."

Owen stared at the smoldering phone for a moment then slid a little farther from the fire. He scooped sand into his hands and buried the device until the smoke stopped seeping from it.

"Hey, sorry about your interweb." Relic's voice was deep and sincere. "It was like your face was glued to it or something."

"I'm the one who dropped it in the fire." Owen stared at the small mound of sand.

"Here…" Relic held out the gin.

Owen sensed an offer of more than just moonshine. He took the flask and two full swallows, relishing the burn, embracing the heat in his belly, a mixture of self-punishment and reward. He held tightly to the container and tried to let the loss of his phone sink in. Damn it.

Owen stared into the crackling flames and felt a weight on his shoulders, a coat of wet concrete, a sense of depression washing over the sideboards. Was he really addicted to the stupid phone, buried in the sand at his feet? How pathetic. Worse yet, did he really just threaten Relic, a man who'd saved his life down by the river, helped him escape, got him food and water, shared his homemade gin? Did he really tell Relic he was a federal officer with the Park Service? He shook his head. What's happening to him? Is it something new, or is he seeing something already there, something about himself that he doesn't really want to know?

He looked up again. The fire flashed its strobe on

Relic's face, lighting cheekbones high and stark, his hair a tangled outline on the night sky, then swirling Relic's eyes deep in moving shadows. A man who thinks the universe is infinite and sacred and that the interweb, as he called it, is a sparkly toy. Bigfoot himself.

"So, how's that cut on your side? Gotta keep it clean…"

Owen pulled his shirt tail partway up, one-handed, and tried to examine it in the firelight. "OK I guess. Not bleeding." He lowered his shirt and sighed, then returned the moonshine to Relic, who took a pull.

"Finish it up." Relic handed it back.

Owen poured the last of the gin down his throat and coughed.

"It doesn't look like a normal cut. It's more like something grazed your skin, just there," he pointed above Owen's hip. "But don't let a wound like that worry you. In fact, I know guys who'd kill for a bullet wound, a scar to impress everybody you tell about it."

"How do you know it's from a bullet?"

"Could be…"

"A bullet wound is a good thing?"

"When you survive it is, and it leaves a good, solid scar like that one will. The girls will love it." Relic's smile gleamed in the firelight.

Owen huffed.

"No, really. You were flying in a tiny plane, just a dot across the vast desert…" Relic stretched his arm smoothly in front of him, mimicking the flight of the Cessna. "Protecting those young college girls…"

Owen grinned.

Relic leaned forward. "You know: wounded Park Ranger flies onward."

The smile slipped from Owen's face. "But I can't fly a damn thing." He shook his head and felt the ground sway a bit beneath him.

"Owen, I think you're pretending you can't do something you really can. Look, there are actual limits in the world, then there are the ones we put on ourselves, the ones that come from what we think. They're like little tape recordings, circling and circling around," he spun his finger in the air. "Voices in our heads."

"Voices?"

"Yep. People walk around all day with them, crap others have drilled into them. Somebody's told you you're not good enough, you can't do something or other, and you're repeating it to yourself. Someone's keeping you grounded when you know damn well you can fly."

Relic's choice of words seemed to echo through

him and he found himself puzzling for a moment. He tried to shake free of it.

"Everything we are arises from our thoughts." Relic pointed to his own head.

Owen grunted.

"So, ask yourself…where did that thought come from? Who said it to you? Somebody put in in your head. Even if it's from a parent, a teacher, or friend, if it's holding you back, why should you listen to it? Why would you grab a handful of shit and inhale?" He cupped his hand to his nose and sniffed an exaggerated breath. "Expose the falsehoods for what they are, then, dump 'em out." He turned his palm upside down, as if to empty it.

"It's not that easy…"

"You're exactly right about that. Your biggest battles in life will be with yourself. But you have to start there." Relic lifted a twig and poked the fire, freeing hot embers to drift and swirl in the air. "Think about your point of view, and try another one on for size. Einstein said, 'When you change the way you look at things, the things you look at change.'"

Owen felt the gin pumping through his brain and thought about Einstein, and Relic, and mutations in a person's point of view. He looked out beyond the sandstone ridges that framed the night sky and realized he was seeing the heart of the Milky Way, millions of suns and moons and planets billions of miles and years away but as solid and real and illuminating as the little campfire at his feet. He added wood to the fire and watched as the flames flickered through dry branches, steadily rooting into the old driftwood. The blaze itself seemed random, brightening and dimming, expanding and contracting when it felt like it, all the while glimmering with an immutable combustion, the same magical conversion of matter into energy that governed the stars themselves.

Owen then remembered the police reports he'd heard: sightings of someone suspicious, a man with a black ponytail, and the reward. Owen stared at the dust at his feet, remembering that moment in the canyon below, embarrassed at his feeble effort to pretend he had a gun hidden behind his back, to be a ranger in charge, a cop dealing with a suspect. But he wasn't quite sure what else to do.

"Technically, I'm supposed to make you my prisoner."

"Fine by me," Relic smiled. "We've got more important things to worry about. Like what's going on back at the students' camp. We need to warn them, help them get out of there."

Right, the students, Owen thought. What were they going to do about them? "Hey…do you have any weapons with you?"

"My slingshot," Relic patted a pocket on his pants. "Why?"

"Well, a pistol would've been good. Those guys at the dig site have guns. Luke…he's gotta be the man who shot me and Thomas down…"

"Shot the engine, too, it looks like. Saw smoke coming from it as you went down along the cliffs. And who knows what he might do with those college kids back there, at the dig site."

CHAPTER 31

"Wanna rum and coke?" the girl's arm wandered a bit as she handed Suzy a plastic glass, not waiting for a reply.

"Well…"

"Wendy's getting shum music on her computer, shum stuff she downloaded before we left civilishation…"

"Uh, huh." Suzy took the cup.

"Then we'll get thish party roll'n," she spun on her foot, lost and caught her balance, and weaved her way across the open area between the campfire and student tents.

"I'd say the party's already started," Suzy said to herself. She listened to the disconnected conversations pulsing through the camp and took a sip. She could see movement inside the big tents where she was headed, hoping to learn more about why Everett and his group were bringing boxes to the dig after the students left the site each day. If she got caught eavesdropping, maybe she could pretend to be drunk, disoriented.

"Hey, I hoped to find you here!" Balancing his drink, Bruce pulled a chair close to her and leaned against it. His teeth shined in the light of the fire, his lips exaggerated and lopsided.

"Uh…"

"They had enough water, so they let us take a sponge bath tonight…"

"Yeah, I…"

"Felt great. Water's warm. You could take one, too, if you want," he pointed toward the larger tents, the ones Suzy wanted to reach. But not with Bruce around.

"No, thanks."

"I could show you…" he leaned forward. "Help you out, if you like." His fingers touched her arm and she pulled away.

"Hey, is that any way to be?" His lips tightened. "I'm just joking around."

"OK, but no sponge bath for me, thanks." She began to leave.

"Wait," he reached for her again.

She stepped away. "Not in the mood, Bruce."

His eyes narrowed. The side of his face blushed

warm, his nose and chin deeply angular in the flickering firelight, his jaw clenched, the vessels in his neck throbbing.

No one else was nearby.

She'd met men like him before. Clean-cut, pleasant-sounding guys with angry hearts just under the surface, safe until they were drunk, when the monster slid from under its veneer. She shivered and began to walk away, willing herself to relax, to keep her gait steady. Bruce blocked her path back to the big tents used by Everett and the others, so she moved toward the camp kitchen.

As she made her way toward the food table, she heard the scrape of shoes on dirt and glanced back. Damn it. Bruce was following her. She scurried to a trash bag tied to the table and tossed her drink into it. She kept her gaze down and watched her own feet move farther from the kitchen and the campfire and into the dark, not sure what else to do at that moment.

He was drunk, she thought, but lazy and tired. He would not follow her far.

She increased her pace as she neared the creek and the blackened shadows of the boxelder trees. She no longer heard him but sensed he was still following at a distance. She wound her way through some tall sage and into the trees, feeling her way as she went, moving toward the gentle gurgle of the creek. The stream opened before her and she hopped across, relieved to have placed some kind of boundary between them. She continued to brush against the trees but soon found herself beyond them, back in the open plain again. She turned to look behind her.

Bruce must have stopped at the edge of the trees. She listened carefully and heard only some distant rustling, maybe Bruce turning back to camp. Then, a splash in the water, a misplaced step, and she knew he was coming across the creek. A bolt of alarm flashed up her spine.

"Should've stayed closer to camp," she whispered, then thought to make her way back, re-cross the stream farther down, and get others to help her. Angela should be back in her tent by now too, and she was responsible for the welfare of the students. Probably had pepper spray for just such occasions, if it came to that.

Suzy saw Bruce's shadow appear from behind the trees sooner than she'd expected. She braced herself.

"Hey," he jogged then reached his arm toward her, closer than she liked. She turned and ran down stream, determined to find a place to cross back toward the camp, when a lanky man stepped in front of her and she skidded to a stop.

Luke.

"What are you doing?" he asked.

Bruce could be heard closing in on them.

"Just need to get back to camp." Her words took the last of the air from her lungs and she gasped for more, angry at herself for being out of breath. She stepped to the side of Luke and watched as Bruce came near.

"You – back to camp!" Luke spoke firmly to Bruce and unshouldered his rifle.

Bruce came to a full stop. "Well, sure, there, Luke. Just getting some fresh air."

"Plenty of it back at camp too."

"Sure." Bruce glared at Suzy for a moment and turned to make his way back toward the creek.

Suzy took a deep breath and nodded at Luke.

"Don't be going up to those ruins," Luke pointed toward the cliff behind him.

"No, no, I'm headed back right now," she pointed in the other direction, downstream from where Bruce was headed.

"Wouldn't want you to get hurt out here." His voice turned deep and he adjusted the Winchester in his hands. "They say that place is haunted."

She nodded again, eyeing the rifle.

"I'm not joking."

"No, of course not. The place is haunted." She took a half step back.

"No, I'm gonna prove it's *not* haunted. But I did see something up there, myself, just the other day," he stepped toward her. "Middle of the day, too. Looked me right in the eye, and when I looked away, it was gone."

"Spooky," she volunteered.

"Yepper. Spooky's not the half of it. Until I can get to the bottom of it, we all need to stay careful around here."

"No doubt," she agreed, wondering whether she'd been safer around Bruce, the drunk.

Luke took a step closer.

CHAPTER 32

"Thanks! I promise to stay clear of the ruins." Suzy's voice rose an octave as she stepped away from Luke and lifted her hand, a quick wave, a quick message that she did not need his help, and she turned and trotted toward the creek again, worried that Luke would keep talking if she dallied.

She moved downstream from where Bruce had wandered back to camp and found a gap in the trees. She moved to the bubbling water and took three deep breaths, slowing them each time, working to release the tension Bruce and Luke had created. A twitch ran through her fingers as she considered the risks she'd faced. Unnecessary risks. She'd be better prepared next time, smarter about dealing with it. She inhaled the deep, cool air and hopped across the creek.

The day's ambient light had long since faded, the

world transformed into blobs of gray and black. She moved into the open, toward the students' camp, and could see the fire clearly, cartoonish shadows dancing past the strobing flames in spurts and stops.

The sky above the plateau had begun to fill with specks of silver light, distant stars revealing themselves to the canyon. She knew the plain was level here, sage and bundles of grass rising from the soil, living hair on the face of the earth. She walked casually toward the large tents where Everett and Luke and the other guy stayed, angling away from the students and, hopefully, Bruce. Maybe Angela was still up there, cataloging the day's finds, and she could strike up a conversation, see what the archeological reports looked like, avoid the partyers until they'd all collapsed. Maybe get a clue about what the owner's representatives were doing at the dig after the students were done each day.

She walked toward the big tents and the hangar, but stayed outside the light of the campfire. Bruce was staggering toward a seated group, grinning foolishly, a drink in each hand. He didn't see her.

Suzy made her way past the students and found a small trail that led across the field. Lanterns glowed inside the owners' tents like beacons, outposts on another world. She sensed movement inside the nearest canvas and heard voices floating on the air like recordings played too slowly. She decided not to try to eavesdrop, choosing instead to get some help.

"Hey, Angela! Is Angela still here?" Suzy kept a steady pace toward the nearest shelter. Sounds within the tent stopped.

"Angela?" she repeated.

"Yes?" Silhouettes moved through each other like ghosts in a flurry of confusing movement. "Is that you, Suzy?"

"Yes." She stopped in front of the tent flap and crossed her hands in front of her. "Sorry to disturb you, but…"

"No disturbance," Angela pulled back the flap, her chest and head backlit by bright lanterns. "Come in."

Suzy stepped into the light and blinked as she adjusted to the glare.

"We were just finishing up for the night." Angela pointed to a portable table set in the middle of the tent, one lantern there, another on the ground toward the back.

"Good to see you again, Suzy," Everett waved and knelt to dim the lower lantern.

"What can I do for you?" Angela stood in front of the table-top. Grainy photographs of the site were spread across the table with a bundle of daily logs. Everett loaded something into a cardboard box on the ground.

"Just wanted to avoid the crowd tonight…" Suzy pushed her fingertips into her pockets.

"Getting a little out of hand, is it?"

"Well, to be honest, I was hoping to talk with you about something…"

"Everett, I'm going to step out with Suzy and we can talk again tomorrow." Angela pointed Suzy toward the exit.

"No problem. We'll see you tomorrow." Everett stood and slipped on his best smile.

Suzy and Angela left the tent and moved a few feet away.

"What's up?"

"Well, I kind of hate to raise it, in case it's just the alcohol talking, but you know Bruce…"

Angela put her hands on her hips. "Yes?"

"I've been really nervous around him. I've made it clear I'm not interested in the guy but tonight he followed me out of camp, out past the creek. I ran into Luke…"

"…Luke…"

"Who kinda helped me out, told Bruce to go

home for the night. So I just want to alert you to this. I don't want to make any formal complaint, but in case I can't handle it, I want you to be aware of the problem."

"You did the right thing. Do you have pepper spray or anything?"

"No."

"I've got something that will do. I'll get it for you when we get to our camp." She turned back toward the tent and stuck her head inside.

"Everett, be a honey and remind us to talk tomorrow about an issue with one of my male students…"

"Sure," Everett replied from inside the tent.

"Maybe you or Luke could have a word with him…"

"Sure thing."

Angela lingered for another moment, some other communication moving between them, it seemed, then turned back to Suzy.

"Let's get back to our tents and I'll get you my little stun gun."

Suzy's eyes widened.

"Well, I'm responsible for your safety in this class…and I've just expanded field archeology to include a bit of self-defense." She put her arm around Suzy's shoulder and they walked together down the trail.

In the moment, she forgot to ask about Everett and the other men with boxes at the dig site.

CHAPTER 33

Everett pushed the wire-rimmed glasses higher on his nose. Angela had left with Suzy about twenty minutes earlier and he hoped she would return alone but, as time ticked by, that seemed less and less likely, and it irked him. He and Angela were done with their inventory for the night, but he'd had a lot more than that in mind for the evening.

Heavy footsteps approached the outside of the tent. Everett turned back to the file folders on the table, quickly all business-at-hand.

Luke swept back the tent flap and looked around. "How's it going?"

Everett distributed one folder into each of the numbered boxes laid out beneath the table. "Fine. How are things outside?"

"Good. Just riding herd, but geez, for college kids,

those guys can be pretty stupid…"

"Oh?" Talk about the pot calling the kettle black, he thought.

"Annoying, too. Drunks chasing babes through the dark, out there playing games, running around like idiots. I feel like a fucking babysitter."

"Well, you've got a lot more common sense than what a couple of college classes can teach you." Everett's affect was smooth.

"I sure as shit hope so…need a hand there?"

"Sure, thanks. Start taping these boxes up for us, will you?"

Luke found the strapping tape and kneeled to the first one. A sound like ripping paper filled the tent as he tore the first stretch of tape from the roller.

"Twenty-four boxes this time," Everett said.

"Good number." Luke tore another length of tape.

"I have to ask you…"

Luke looked up at Everett.

"Has Johnson been acting a little weird lately?"

"Well…"

"Ever since he got back from his last run to town, he's been on edge, I'd say, maybe even shaky."

"I hadn't noticed. He can get a little cocky…"

Luke flattened tape onto the first box.

"All hat and no cattle, huh?" Everett smiled.

"Yeah, he likes playing cowboy. Makes him feel in charge or something."

"It's stupid, really." Everett walked to the side of the table.

"Stupid," Luke agreed.

"Yeah, but…"

The sound of peeling tape interrupted him. Luke looked up again. "Sorry. What?"

"I need to be serious for a minute, here. Johnson is beginning to freak me out a little bit."

Luke put down the tape and stood up.

"You're not seeing it?" Everett squinted.

"Maybe…"

"Look, I hate to tell you this," Everett waved his hand toward Luke, "but Johnson thinks you're dumb as a post."

"What?" Luke stepped closer to Everett, his face reddened. "He said that?"

"He used those very words." Everett looked at his feet and shook his head.

"That shithead…"

"He doesn't respect either one of us, Luke," he looked up again, "and it's even worse than that."

"What?"

"I don't know…" Everett raised and lowered his arms. "Maybe it's just me…but I don't think so anymore. We both have to be on our toes around Johnson now. I don't think he'd hesitate to plug a hole in us with that six shooter of his."

Luke's mouth hung open, posing the question, "Why?"

"Because he's been dealing behind our backs during these deliveries. He wants us to lower our prices. He's renegotiating, damn it, making some kind of side deal for himself. Kickbacks."

"Really? Shit."

"That's gotta be it." Everett rubbed his hand across his forehead and stared at the table. "He came back from his last trip all nervous, sweaty even, explained how the dealer was paying too much, can you believe it?" He glanced at Luke. "The dealer paying us too much!"

"Shit." Luke plucked the cap from his head and held it tightly in his fist.

"And he kept fiddling with his pistol, made me nervous as hell."

"Cocky ass-wipe."

"He said he'd already agreed to discount the load,

see, so I had no choice but to go along with it, but then I realized I'd better stop arguing about it…"

"Damn it to hell."

"I know, Luke, I know." Everett shook his head. "I had to get this off my chest. At least I feel better telling you all this, knowing we're both forewarned…"

"What are we gonna do?" Luke's hands began crumpling his hat.

"We have to be ready to defend ourselves. Ready to shoot back, if we have to."

Luke stared at the boxes on the ground, the tent quiet as a classroom during final exams.

"What are you thinking?" Everett stepped closer to him.

Luke patted the rifle on his shoulder. "The best defense is a good offense."

Everett stopped and took a half step back. "Shit. Really?"

Luke straightened.

Everett stared at Luke for a moment and looked to the ground, rubbing his chin. "That's dangerous talk."

Luke nodded.

"Look, I don't want this, but, if it comes to it…if you have to take him out, you should have his share of the profits."

Luke's eyes widened.

"Really, I mean think about it. You've been doing all the heavy lifting around here, taking care of those delinquents, shooting that plane out of the air, protecting all of us. If you have to take out Johnson, well, that protects me, too. You do that," Everett looked into Luke's eyes and pointed at him, "and his share is all yours, one hundred percent."

Luke tightened his lips into a hard line, but the edges crept into a little smile.

CHAPTER 34

Maybe it was the buzzing gin, the deep fatigue, or the smoldering phone at his feet, but something restless shifted in Owen's chest. He stood and gathered his balance. He could feel Relic's gaze on him but said nothing. Owen turned and walked away from their little fire, beyond its flickering glow and into the desert night.

At first, his head filled with thoughts of his old job at Williamsburg, his old girlfriend Lisa, her father, his old probation officer, Pete. Then he remembered Thomas and shuddered, from the image of his leaden face, a cool gust across the flats, or both. He wrapped his arms around his stomach.

Owen scuffled his tired feet over the rocks and across the sand. Ahead lay a darkness as deep as he'd ever imagined, a wall of cliff that blocked the light of the stars. The canyon opened to his left, the galaxy a thickened luster smeared across obscurity. His feet smacked on something hard and he looked down along a long slab of stone, bare in the thin light of the cosmos. He stopped and stood, the night air unspeaking and motionless as outer space.

He thought about what Relic had said, about the voices in our heads, and it didn't seem as crazy as it had at first. It was tied to the other idea about which point of view we adopt and which we don't. Our perspective on things could be deeply twisted, even if there are some hard facts to support it. He remembered the story of the elephant, the old saying about seeing it as a tree, if you find only its leg, or as a hose if you find only its trunk. The whole beast seemed designed by a gaggle of gnomes. But it was actually a single conglomerate of bone, muscle, and consciousness, driven by a spirit of determination.

Now he knew. He's been stuck on the elephant's leg, stopping there, reaching conclusions about a shackled future, giving up on his own imagination, never having felt the miraculous trunk, the magnificent flapping ears. And it was the voices that stopped him, a chorus just under the surface, vague, slippery, hard to grab, harder to choke off. The ones he listened to all the time, the ones telling him to wrestle into a mold, a suit of clothes too tight in the chest, too long in the legs. The ones telling him he "can't" change, explore, expand. Well, if he listens to them, he thought, they will be right.

He sucked a deep breath of cool air and tried to clear his mind.

Pools of water, collected from the recent rain, filled potholes in the sandstone terrace. He stared at the largest one, six feet to his left, and his eyes refocused away from the rough land, toward the smooth bath, into what the puddle reflected. Suddenly he was seeing the heart of the Milky Way again, billions of stars not soaring through space above him but immersed in the tiny pool, halos cast at unfathomable distances all right here, caught in an intimate sheen of water at his very feet.

He moved closer to the shallow pocket of water and squatted at its edge. He stared downward, seeing upward, into the lights of the night sky, proof that the rest of the universe was not empty, proof that it was speaking to him after all and it all floated in a living mirror within reach of his fingertips. He reached out to touch the surface then pulled back quickly, afraid he might disturb the glimmer, the medicine of it, soothing his wounds, sweeping all the puzzles into a new perspective, loosening his own.

Owen rested there for quite a while, empty of words and memories, his chest feeling every breath. When a discomfort in his tired legs grew to distraction, he stood and shuffled back to the dimming fire.

"Relic, I want you to know something…"

Relic tossed another stick onto the flames.

"I'm ready. I'm ready to go now…"

Relic met his gaze head-on and nodded. "Then tomorrow's gonna be a tough day. We'll both need our rest tonight. Take this," he tossed Owen a rain parka from his pack. "Get some shut eye."

Owen slipped into the parka and curled up on the sand to sleep, fewer voices in his head.

CHAPTER 35

Their little alcove looked very different in the morning light, no longer a colorless shadow above them. The makeshift camp was set in a tilted bowl of rock gouged from the ochre cliff, glowing now like a fiery ember tossed from the rising sun. His sleep had been fierce, driven by exhaustion and injury, welcoming even a bed of sand. Owen lay in a fetal position for a while longer, blinking away the sleep, curling tighter then straightening and rolling onto his back.

He could hear Relic moving about, zipping something on his pack, boots scraping against the rock.

"You OK?" Relic asked.

"Humph." Owen stared at the pale sky along the distant cliffs and relished the feel of his muscles at rest, immobile and relaxed. He knew they would have to move on and part of him resented it. He rolled onto his side and pushed himself to a seated position across from Relic.

Relic's hair was neatly combed into a tight pony tail, his thin goatee clean and straight. A few tiny streaks of gray made his night-black hair seem even darker. He'd rolled his shirt sleeves up past his elbows, looking relaxed and ready to go.

"Here. Breakfast." Relic tossed him a baggie filled with hard, round objects, colored in blues and reds and greens. "Chocolate for energy, peanuts for protein."

Owen opened the bag of M&Ms.

"Keep that bag, and pace yourself. Eat a few at a time." Relic tossed Owen his water bottle. "But drink all the water you can hold."

Owen popped six of the candies into his mouth and savored them as if he'd never eaten anything so sweet before in his life.

"Staying hungry makes a man appreciate the finer things in life..." Relic grinned, crossed his legs and leaned back on his arms.

Owen finished the food faster than he wanted and washed the sugar from his throat with plenty of water. He slid out of Relic's parka and handed it to him.

"The rifleman took the easy way back, out in the open. We'll have to go the long way and it'll take us most of the day. But we'll get to Ghost Creek by evening." Relic reached for the water bottle. "We'll go north from here, stay out of the lower canyons. There's a place we can cross to the other drainage, where the creek begins, at a spring above where the students are digging."

Owen nodded.

"Who did you talk to down there at the dig site, when you flew in with Thomas?"

"We met with a woman named Angela, I think, who's their professor, or aide, somebody from the college, I'm sure." Owen shifted his legs in front of him. "A student named Suzy was with her, and they both showed Thomas around the site. I also met Everett and saw a guy with a rifle, who pulled Everett away from me to talk for a while. That's when I wandered around and found the…body, the…arm sticking out of the dirt."

"I've seen the rifleman up close. You can bet your ass he's the one who shot you out of the sky." Relic stood and carried the water bottle to the white plastic bucket anchored below the rim of their camp. He tilted the last of the rainwater into the bottle, then carefully repositioned the bucket and the large rock inside it. Ingenious, Owen thought. At the next rain, he'd have a full bucket again.

Owen shifted his position, easing some of the stiffness in his muscles. "Makes sense. He was the only one I saw with any kind of weapon. But what the hell are they doing down there? Why would they kill a girl and bury her?"

"Girl?"

"It was definitely a woman's hand. And she had nail polish on her fingers."

Relic nodded.

"One of the students?" Owen asked.

"I doubt it. If she was with the students, someone would have raised an alarm…" Relic lifted his index finger.

"Have you been watching them? Is that how you saw me and Thomas in the plane?" Owen sealed the bag of M&M's and tucked them into his pants pocket.

"With all the noise and campfires and truck traffic, you can't hardly miss this crew. The three stooges, I call 'em, stay in the big tents by the hangar. The students are scattered around closer to the creek. I haven't seen so much commotion there in a long time, since the feds first excavated around the ruins."

"The ones in the cliffs above the creek?"

Relic nodded and tucked the water into his pack. He walked back to Owen and sat down again.

"Whatever it is, I don't think all those students would be in on it. I think they're some sort of cover for what's really going on." Relic stared across the sage-dotted meadow.

"Which is why we need to warn them, get them out of there." Owen gently rubbed the shallow wound on his side.

"You'll need to find this Angela and Suzy." Relic stroked his goatee. "They'll remember you, they'll listen to you, if you can warn them. They'll have to help us figure out a way to get the students out of there safely. We may need a diversion too. Let's think about this while we hike." He rose smoothly and turned toward his pack.

"Right." Owen leaned on his right arm and scooted his feet underneath him, standing slowly, feeling aches in every joint, sinew pulled beyond its comfort. He stretched his back and shook out his fingers. His knees weakened and he quickly straightened, locking them beneath his weight. Maybe once he started moving, he could keep going, make it to their destination without embarrassing himself.

It's a theory at least, he thought.

CHAPTER 36

He followed Relic at a steady pace through some of the strangest country he'd ever seen. "Hoodoos," Relic called them: dollops of wet summer sand three stories high, dropped and stacked on themselves by some giant child a million years ago, striped in shades of brass and ash, dried hard and bald in the desert sun. Narrow game trails weaved their way across open ground, skirting beds of prickly pear cactus, winding between tough branches of sage, leading them toward distant cliffs of terra cotta sandstone.

The sun baked every ounce of moisture from everything, it seemed, and even the sweat on his back dried before it dampened his shirt. But the dry air made every rock and bush and shadow clear and stark, like it was right before him even when it was miles away. Colors bubbled to the surface under that burning glow, tomato red, sandstone bronze, the vibrant green of spring grass. He'd never been surrounded by sky so rich a shade of purple-blue, a deep translucence you could see and sense and breathe, a canopy that faded into infinite space, that proved the existence of the third dimension on so grand a scale.

They walked and walked, over hard-baked ground, shifting sand, slabs of sandstone, the pace steady and tough, until Owen lost track of time. Eventually, his stomach stopped grumbling and he forgot how sore his muscles had been when they'd begun.

After a while, Relic moved to the shade of a hoodoo and slid his pack to the ground. He'd finished a deep drink of water by the time Owen arrived.

"You OK?" He handed the water to Owen.

"Yeah." Owen nearly finished the bottle.

"Save a little, for now. We'll reach the spring in another couple of hours."

"Over there?" Owen pointed to a wall of chiseled cliff.

Relic turned to look. "Near there, along the base."

Owen nodded and handed the water back to Relic, who stuffed it into his pack. Relic flipped his ponytail clear of his shirt collar and the motion triggered a memory. That discussion in the sheriff's office about a wanted man…

"Let's sit for a while." Relic put one foot over the other, lowered himself, and sat on the ground cross-legged. "Take a rest in this shade."

Owen squatted awkwardly and plopped into the dust. For just a moment, he felt the urge to turn on his cell phone, scroll across the busy pages, take his mind somewhere other than where he was. But his phone was toast. Can he live without instant news and twitter and email and the "interweb," as Relic calls it? Can anyone turn it off, when they should? And why does Relic go without it?

"You live out here, all of the time?"

"Mostly, sure." Relic's eyes seemed to ask if that was the only question Owen had.

"Well, I just wondered, I mean, it's stunning out here. Way different from the humidity of Virginia…"

Relic seemed only partially satisfied by Owen's answer, but he didn't press it. "It's not just the country that's unique, but the people who've lived in it, for centuries."

"I can see why you like being out here." Owen nodded and took a deep breath.

"You can pray in temples built by people or in temples built by the Creator." Relic nodded toward a row of hoodoos striped in shades of cinnamon and flour, calloused sandstone fingers reaching upward.

Owen stared at the procession of standing rocks. "I can see your point. And there's a lot more history here than I thought too."

"The land shapes the people, you know, whoever they are, their history, their character, their relationship with creation."

"Yes." Owen scanned the northern cliffs.

"And the people live on, on the mesas southeast of here, Hopi and Zuni, Acoma and Laguna, and all the others, as strong as ever…"

Owen looked back at Relic.

"Here, history stretches not just two hundred years, but twenty thousand. The past is never fully behind us, out of reach. It's with us all the time, on a continuum that's back there but also here and now, a bridge you can reach across and touch. And all of this," he swung his arm toward the horizon, "is shaping us, our thoughts, our perceptions, just like it shaped the Pueblo people, the Old Ones, them and us, then and now."

Owen considered that.

Relic stared out across the horizon then leaned against the curving hoodoo and closed his eyes.

Owen pondered what Relic had said, the full

breadth of human culture, language, ceremonies, from here to Siberia to Egypt, all with the same innate need for food, shelter, family, passion, self-growth. On a grand scale, it seemed like each generation had to re-learn it all, a massive shame that humanity had to try over and over again, gaining ground, losing ground, repeating history, as they say. On the other hand, the phenomenon had its own value, an unfathomable blessing that humanity got to experience over and over again, fresh to each new generation. Maybe that's why we have to die, he thought, lamenting Thomas' slumped shoulders, his ashen face. So we can return to the world with fresh eyes and passion and lust, recycled, to take the journey again. It's all in your perspective.

Owen looked to his feet and shuffled them. Relic seemed fully relaxed, his head rested on the rock, eyes still closed. Owen let his mind drift through random ideas and recent events.

The ponytail, Owen suddenly thought, that's what sparked his earlier notion…and now he knew it was a different question than the one he'd asked. Is Relic the mystery man the sheriff's deputy and all the others in the meeting had talked about? If he's the guy, then he's a criminal, a fugitive, so, no…it can't be true. But how many back-country hermits could there be? A low voice mumbled in the back of his head again, warning him, telling him what Probation Officer Pete would do, what his old girlfriend's father would do. Turn Relic in to the police? Get a hand on that reward? Earn himself a promotion?

Owen thought back to the law enforcement briefing, the joking reference to Bigfoot, and smiled to himself. That's more like it, he decided. Nothing sinister here, just "sightings" of Relic blown into mythical proportions. There's no reward for finding Bigfoot, except the find itself. He stretched his neck backwards, gazing toward the top of the sandstone hoodoo and dozed.

After a time, Owen heard Relic moving.

"Daylight's wasting." Relic stood and pulled the rucksack onto his shoulders. He smiled and turned toward the open ground, the length of his ponytail draped across his pack.

CHAPTER 37

Owen and Relic walked across the long flats in relative silence, picking their way around rocks and saltbush, scrambling across inclines, lowering themselves down sandstone ridges. Shadows began to spread across the little valley they'd entered, exaggerating the heights and shapes of cliffs above them. Rather suddenly, the ground levelled out. A tub-sized pool of water bubbled in the center of it all, cattails stiff and erect, guarding the edges, lush grasses, curved at the tops, wild hairs growing out of the ground.

"This is the spring?" Owen searched for a rock to sit on.

"Yep. I'll fill up the bottles, then we can make our way downstream."

Owen found a seat and stretched his legs. He reached in his pants pocket for the baggie of M&M's

and finished the last of them. Eating them only made him hungrier.

They appeared to be in another box canyon, but the ledges above them showed ways to the top, and he'd learned that looks could be deceiving out here. He rolled his neck and arms then stared into the sky. A lone raven squawked his alarm and rode a thermal wind rising along the cliffs. Owen began to feel his legs stiffen, so he stood and shook them out. They both drank all they could, Relic refilled the bottle again and they began a trek across the bottom of the canyon. From here, at least, the going would be downhill.

It took them another hour-and-a-half to reach a spot where the canyon widened and the stream, also fed by a couple of smaller springs, began to gather speed. From here, Owen could see the brown Colorado River in the distance, a ribbon of life clinging to its moisture.

They walked along the creek more slowly now, stopping frequently to scan the horizon and search for the archeological dig and the college tents. In another half-hour, they rounded a gentle bend in the creek and saw the students, all lined up at a table near a large canopy. Someone appeared to be serving food as people made their way through the line and into separate camp chairs, arranged in a semi-circle nearby. Now and then, solitary words floated across the valley with the clink of metal pots and forks.

"Will you recognize the women you met the other day?" Relic stepped into shadow.

"If I can get closer, yeah."

"See the rifleman or any of his buddies?"

"No."

"Keep a keen eye out and let's move closer."

CHAPTER 38

They made their way downstream, keeping the creek between them and the student camp. When they were only a couple of hundred yards away, one of the students began walking toward them, her eyes on the ruins, to the north and above them.

Relic put his hand on Owen's shoulder and pulled him into a crouching position next to bushes along the water.

"Hey, I think that's her." Owen pointed.

"Talk to her. Warn them. I'm going to reconnoiter a bit, see if I can figure out where the rifleman is patrolling. Meet you back here in a while." Relic turned and scooted away, keeping low to the ground.

The young woman – Suzy – stopped, hooked her thumbs in her belt, and stared at the ancient ruins. Owen took a deep breath, stood, and dusted himself off. He hopped across the stream and began to walk directly toward her.

She stood there impassively for a moment, then turned to watch Owen as he approached. Her eyes showed some concern at first and then surprise.

"Hey, Suzy, you remember me?"

"Yes. Owen, is it?"

"Yeah. We need to talk for a minute…" he strode to about eight feet away and stopped. "We have to talk. Can we do that?"

"Sure."

He glanced at a tear in his loose shirt tail and at his dusty boots, dog-tired and worn. He realized what he must look like: a cave man covered in dried mud and sand and sweat, a wandering fool with a barbaric story. Owen sat in the dust by a patch of grass and slowly crossed his legs. Suzy moved closer and sat across from him, her expression full of questions.

"Thanks for sitting. My legs are pretty stiff."

"Why are you here? I thought you and the pilot flew off a long time ago." She leaned forward, eyes narrowing.

"I have a lot to tell you, so I'd best get right to it. You know the guy around here with the rifle? Skinny guy who sort of patrols here?"

"Luke."

"Him, yeah. Well…he shot our plane out of the sky with that rifle. We crashed in the river, south of here. Thomas, the pilot, is dead. I've been walking to get back here ever since, to warn you and the other students. I don't know what the hell is going on but no one is safe here."

Her eyes opened wide and she expelled a blast of air. "What?"

Owen nodded and looked directly at her. "It's true. I would never believe it myself, but that guy, Luke, shot us up. The plane's in the river now and," he glanced at his feet, "Thomas is still in there, too."

"Holy…"

"I figured you and Angela were the ones to talk to about this."

"Shit, Owen…" she shook her head and kneaded her hands together. "Damn."

"Yeah."

"You survived and made it all the way back to warn us?"

"I had some help, a guy named…" Owen realized he'd begun to think of Relic as the kind of person he could rely on. "A friend named Relic."

"Relic?"

"Nickname, I guess. Anyway, he found me along the river and we escaped up another side-canyon."

"Shit."

"Luke chased us up there, shot at us some more, but he missed. Relic knew a way up that Luke didn't have, and we got away, then made our way back here. You've got to let the students know, get them out of here."

Suzy looked into the distance, deep in thought. "I'll get Angela and we'll get a plan together. We can't just tell the students, not yet, or they'll all react at once and Luke and those guys will know something's up. Some of these students could even start a stampede, of sorts. I think there's only one truck here right now that we could use and Everett has the keys."

"Everett?"

"He's the boss, as far as I can tell. There's Everett, Luke, and Johnson."

"Three of them? The rest are students?"

"Yes. And Johnson's on a supply run today, back tomorrow, I think. He has the other truck."

"There's more…" Owen scraped the clay from his fingernails while he thought how best to say it. "There's a body in the dirt behind the hangar. I saw it the day we were here, before Thomas flew us away."

"Oh, god."

"I don't think it's a student, or, obviously, someone with your group would have noticed. I think that's why Luke shot us... They figured out that I'd seen the body. Well, the arm of the body."

Suzy's eyes looked back and forth, her mind moving in thought. "That Luke guy is always shooting targets, for practice. He could have shot someone, and your plane, and none of us would have thought anything about it."

"And he's probably out there right now, patrolling, watching us..."

CHAPTER 39

Owen waited as Suzy took two deep breaths and stared toward the dig site, absorbing the news he had delivered, Owen thought, like a brick through the living room window. But he wasn't sure how else to tell the tale. What Luke, no doubt, had done to the girl with the unburied arm, and what he'd done to Thomas, was too jarring to ease into gently.

After several moments, she turned back to him and he looked up.

"Are you hurt?"

"Mostly sore, and hungry…"

"Oh, shoot, I forgot, I can offer you some food. We just finished and there are extra hamburgers."

As if on cue, his stomach rumbled an answer. "Do we have time?"

"I'll be quick. I'll get you one now…" she stood.

"Two? One for my friend." Owen looked around. "He'll be back soon."

"Yes, of course." She turned.

"Water, too, please…"

She nodded as she rushed back toward the camp kitchen.

He watched her wind her way through the sagebrush and noticed the top of the distant canopy, shaking gently with a gust of wind. He searched all that he could see, recalling the rifle Luke carried on his shoulder, suddenly feeling very exposed. Saltbush, maybe ten feet from where he'd come, grew three or four feet high along the edge of green grass by the little creek. He rose carefully and shuttled himself back to better cover. Human voices swept past him, disconnected words floating like cottonwood seeds blown on the breeze.

He lifted his shirt and examined the "bullet wound," as Relic had called it, and he smiled at the thought it might someday impress a girlfriend. The cause of the long, shallow slice remained a mystery – it may as well be a bullet that did it as a shard of aluminum from the Cessna, or a sharp rock in the river. Redness tinged the edges, but it was no more swollen or tender than it had been the day before. His arms were bruised below the elbows, his hands looked like they'd lost a fight with a cat. His feet ached from the inside out, bones and ankles fatigued beyond what was healthy or safe. He touched his left temple and discovered dried blood, which he peeled from his matted hair. Shit. He must look like hell itself.

Just then, he heard someone walking toward him and he lifted onto his knees, just a bit higher, and waved. Suzy saw him and quickened her pace.

"You moved." She sat in front of him, balancing puffy wraps of tin foil and containers of water. She reached over and handed him the food.

"You're a lifesaver, Suzy." Owen unwrapped the foil to find a steaming hamburger, complete with tomato, lettuce, and mayonnaise, slipped awkwardly out of its hand-squished bun, smelling like an oasis of grease, salt, red meat. He took a large bite, closed his eyes, and suddenly remembered that he had taste buds.

When he looked up, he realized Suzy had been watching him. "Humm?"

"I've been thinking." She shifted closer to him and he found himself liking it. "Angela's our faculty advisor and she'll want to protect the students. She's been in the work-tent Everett uses, and I've seen how he looks at her. Angela's pretty, and a bit of a flirt, and Everett's sweet on her. If anybody can get the truck keys from Everett, it's Angela."

Owen swallowed and reached for the water. "Steal the truck? Get the students in it and take off?"

Suzy nodded.

Owen took a long drink and reached for another bite of the hamburger. "But what the hell is really going on out here? I mean, what are Everett and Luke and this Johnson guy doing that would have them shooting people and airplanes out of the sky?" He took another deep bite of his burger.

"It must have something to do with the dig…"

"Hummph."

"I've seen them carry boxes out to the dig at the end of the day, when we're done out there. They must be bringing them from their work-tent to the site, then back again, nearly every night."

Owen swallowed again and looked at her, his question implicit.

"Right. That's all I know and it doesn't make any sense to me."

He took a breath. "But the answer is somewhere in that tent of theirs…"

"Right…" She looked out over the plain. The summer sun lay low on the western cliffs, tugging the day into dusk.

"I'm going to go talk to Angela and see if she can figure it out. We'll come up with a plan and get everyone out of here."

"We need to meet again, so we can work together."

"Yeah. I'll come back later, but it'll be dark soon. I'll bring flashlights."

"OK."

"Will you be all right? And, where will you be?"

"I'll be fine. I've got to find my friend, but we'll be somewhere along the creek. I'll try to stay in this area, generally, but we may have to hide. Luke's out there, somewhere."

"Right. OK. There's one truck in camp. We've either got to steal it tonight, or first thing in the morning, if we're going to get out of here quickly. That Johnson character comes back tomorrow with the other truck, if he follows his pattern."

Owen wondered why Johnson's routine took him out of camp, overnight, then back again.

"Take care." She stood quickly and turned to leave.

"Hey, thank you again."

"Sure. Whistle softly to let me know where you're at."

"Will do." He watched her trot out of sight and missed her company already.

CHAPTER 40

"Cute girl."

The pack plopped heavily onto the ground and Owen's tired muscles twitched involuntarily. "Shit, you scared the hell out of me."

"Show her your bullet wound, yet?" Relic grinned.

"No."

"Well, don't forget…" Relic sat next to Owen in the shade of the tall bush.

"Be nice to me…" Owen handed a foil-wrapped hamburger to Relic.

"I guess I'll have to, now." Relic opened the foil quickly, his eyes like a child's at Christmas.

"I talked to Suzy, and she's going to talk to Angela, the course director from the college, or whatever she is."

Relic looked up from his meal, chewing with a satisfied smile on his face.

"They're going to find a way to get the pick-up truck, see if the students can take it and drive out of here."

"When?" He took another bite.

"Tonight, maybe, or early in the morning. Suzy will come by here again later, so we can figure it out together."

"How many jackasses are we dealing with? Just the three?"

"Yeah. Luke, Everett, who I met, and a guy named Johnson, who's out on a 'run' of some sort."

"Three stooges..."

"Johnson has the other pickup and Suzy expects him back tomorrow sometime. So it's best to get out of here while we only have two of them to avoid."

"I have an idea about the rifleman..." Relic stuffed the last of the hamburger in his mouth.

"Oh?"

Relic raised a finger, asking Owen to wait until he finished.

"Hand me your tin foil..." Relic mumbled and held out his palm.

Owen gave him the crumpled aluminum.

Relic straightened each of the foil wrappers into smooth, flat pieces and folded them neatly. "I'm going to see if I can distract Luke, keep him busy all night. You and the others find a way to deal with the Everett character and then get out as soon as you can. Of course, bring the sheriff back with you. There will be evidence in that big tent of theirs," he nodded in that direction, "so don't let Everett run off with it or destroy it, if you can help it."

Owen nodded and handed Relic the water bottle that Suzy had brought for him. Relic took a long drink and stopped to catch his breath.

"What's your plan?"

Relic took another long drink, finishing the bottle. He wiped his mouth and smoothed his goatee. "The plan, friend, is not to get caught…" He lifted his pack and strapped it on. Owen struggled to stand and Relic helped him up.

"Tired," Owen said.

"Bullet wound," Relic grinned.

Owen chuckled.

The sun dropped well below the line of cliffs downstream from Ghost Creek, indigo drained from the evening sky. Tiny dots of light moved erratically in the distance, flashlights over at the students' camp.

"Be careful," Owen said.

"If you think it will help…"

CHAPTER 41

Relic turned, ran down the stream, and disappeared into shadows that blended with the night.

Now that he was standing, Owen thought it best not sit again for a while – he was too stiff to keep getting up and down. He wandered toward the camp in the dusk, the fading light allaying his fear about being easily seen in the open. The ground seemed different now, more rugged, and he thought he'd be able to avoid the rocks and sage brush, but he was mistaken. His ankles were taking a beating. Maybe Suzy would bring him a lantern.

He knew the creek was to his left and the camp to his right. He made his way slowly in the direction that Suzy would take to return to find him, anxious to hasten their next meeting and do his best to help her and the other students. As he walked downstream, the land evened out and his eyes adjusted to the semi-dark. Eventually, he stood between the creek and the student's camp, where tents appeared and disappeared magically in the uncertain movement of jaundiced lights.

"Hey! What are you doing out here?"

The voice jarred him and he turned to look. A motion in the dark took form and the shadow of a man approached.

"Just out for a walk," Owen said, straining to recognize the voice.

"Not safe out here. Mountain lions." The man came close and turned his flashlight on, aimed at Owen's face.

"I'm going back to camp now." Owen turned away from the glare and began to move away, fear tingling his nerves, something telling him this was the rifleman, the one Relic was going to try to lure away.

"No, I know who you are, and I've got you now, you little shit."

Owen tried to run but Luke gripped the shirt on his back and moved in front of him. Luke raised the barrel of the Winchester to Owen's face.

"Not a word out of you, ass-wipe, or I blast your face off."

"This close to camp?" Adrenalin leaked into his

bloodstream and Owen felt his anger rise.

"Just a cougar, folks, and I took care of it." Luke held his face close to Owen's, a wicked smile on his tightened lips. "Come with me." He turned Owen away from the camp and shoved him forward, forcing him to step ahead, slip on a rock, catch his balance. Luke moved behind him and poked Owen's neck with the barrel of his rifle.

Now Owen was angry with himself for having walked into the open, thinking the darkness shielded him from Luke or Everett, thinking he'd escaped once and for all. Damn it to hell.

Luke stabbed him with the gun barrel at nearly every step as they made their way straight toward the creek. Luke aimed his lantern on the ground ahead of them and then into the trees as they came to the tumbling water.

"Cross the creek here, ass-wipe."

Maybe Relic will hear them or see the glow of Luke's flashlight and help him, Owen thought. He held his arms out for balance and hopped across the small stream. He gained some distance from Luke for a moment, but once Luke was over the creek too, he poked the unyielding barrel into Owen's back again.

"Stop here."

Owen could hear Luke shuffling behind him.

"Go to that tree, over there." Luke pointed his flashlight at a boxelder, its trunk almost as thick as Owen's body. He moved slowly toward it.

"Hands out."

Owen complied, wondering what was next, wondering if he should try to run, thinking that he'd be an easy target.

Luke put the flashlight under his left arm and slung the rifle over his shoulder.

Now, Owen thought, while the rifle was out of Luke's hands… But Luke quickly slid the gun back into his fingers and aimed it at Owen's stomach.

"Here, tie this onto one wrist." Luke tossed him a piece of thick twine. Owen caught it and stared at it for a moment. He began tying the nylon as slowly and as loosely as he dared.

"Back against the tree."

Owen did as he was told.

"Hands behind the tree."

Owen could think of no way out, no way to disobey. He moved his arms to either side of the trunk.

Luke moved behind him, his flashlight bouncing its glare across the ground. He quickly wrapped, then tied, Owen's free hand to the other one, pulling both wrists tightly against the bark.

Owen couldn't move away from the tree.

Luke shuffled to another spot and tugged at what looked at first like a body, but a rigid one, too lightweight to be real. Luke pulled it from behind a tree, the thing lumpy with repairs, and laid it on the ground about twenty feet from Owen. Luke ran his flashlight across the wooden form, a grotesque face with circled eyes, bullet-riddled shirt and jeans, stuffed with rags, what looked like a homemade scarecrow used for target practice.

Owen felt another rise of dread and took deeper breaths, working to keep panic from taking control. Luke moved back in front of him, searching the ground. He found a rock, moved it, and balanced his flashlight against it.

"Time for some more precision shooting…" Luke moved quickly away from Owen, out across the flats and toward the cliff ruins.

The light shone on the middle of Owen's chest and he suddenly understood Luke's plan.

CHAPTER 42

Owen rolled his head, closed his eyes, and moaned, "Aw… shit!"

A trembling swept through his body, knotting his throat. Muscle grated against bone, lungs against heart, a deep sense of horror and dismay he'd never imagined.

He stared at blades of grass illuminated by the flashlight, the slender creations at once neutral and empty, then filled with meaning, waving at him like a welcoming friend, sharing his world with their own way of life, lit by a metallic glow from the lantern. Maybe the last thing he'd ever see in this world. Focusing on them helped him to take a gulp of air.

Luke's footsteps shuffled and faded into the distance and then, it seemed, stopped altogether.

Owen pulled on his ropes, then slid them up and down the back of the tree, rubbing furiously against the bark, hoping to hell he could tear through them in time.

He heard another sound, a scrape on rock in the distant dark, then quiet. Luke was getting ready to fire.

He thought of Suzy and Relic and Thomas and the last few days as one unified event, no before, no after, no more or less, just all of it at once, a single dent on the surface of time. He told himself not to feel remorse, but something pulled it up by the roots anyway, clods of regret all bare and dangling.

He tried to rotate to the opposite side of the tree, but could only get partway around, the rope snagged or tied on a branch beyond his view. He tugged harder at his restraints, frustration and hatred rising from his chest, his face flushing, his lungs burning and he remembered the freedom he'd felt flying with Thomas, moving through the air like a falcon, rising, dipping, turning at will, in whatever direction they wanted.

He stood still for a moment, hearing nothing, and straightened. His fear was a demonic being with its own mind and it boiled rapidly into anger, a torrent of rage at Luke, his power, his arrogance, the students, anyone but himself but then at himself too, threatening to explode his heart. He had to do something.

He took a deep breath and yelled as loudly as he

could: "Anyone who can hear me!" He took another breath. "Luke is going to kill me! Luke is a scared little asshole and he's going to shoot me for target practice! Anyone who can hear me! Stay away! Luke is a killer!"

He felt the sting of dirt strike his face before he heard the crack of the rifle in the air.

"Missed me, you asshole!" he taunted Luke and twisted to his right, making himself as small a target as he could.

The next shot pounded deep into the tree trunk to his left, where he'd stood moments ago, and again the rifle fire followed the explosion of wood by a fraction of a second.

Owen then twisted to his left as far as he could, feeling the rough bark blown apart by the bullet. He screamed again, certain that by now someone from the camp should have noticed.

The tree shook from a glancing blow, the third shot slightly to Owen's right. Luke was adjusting his aim.

Owen moved to his right again, straining on the ropes, his hands numbing from the constriction, reaching in vain to escape the light of the lantern Luke had propped in front of him and suddenly realized that the lantern, the light that shined up at him, could be moved if he could find a way. He saw a stone by his foot, wiggled the edge of his boot beneath it and yanked upward as fast as he could, spinning the rock toward the light and clean over the top of it.

Splinters blew from the tree above him, whipping tiny darts into his scalp and he yelped in pain and surprise. He searched for another stone, lined his toes against it, and lobbed it against the flashlight, tumbling it from its position, spinning the targeting glow away from him and into the brush.

"Hey!" Suzy's voice rose through the dark. "Hold still!"

Owen felt his hands separate behind the tree, suddenly cut loose from his bind. He spun to his left and away from the trunk as he heard another shot crease through the air and into the tree. Luke could still hit him, but now Owen was just a ghost along the creek and the tree was no longer his captor, but his shield. He reached forward in the dark and found Suzy's arm. She tugged him away and they were soon across the creek, hidden in the deeper shadows.

CHAPTER 43

Relic placed a flat stone in the middle of the doorway of a room in the ruins above the creek and laid twigs he'd brought with him into a square pattern, log cabin style, around loose brush in the center. He moved to the upper window of a ruin about thirty feet away and built a similar structure of kindling atop the edge of the pieces of foil that had held the hamburgers. When the sticks and old leaves were ready, he folded the foil upward, blocking the kindling from view by anyone in the fields below the cliff. Using some loose stones, he anchored the foil around the branches.

He heard the sharp blast of a rifle and knew it was Luke's. He had to hurry.

He lit the window fire behind the tinfoil then ran to the unshielded kindling in the doorway.

A second shot echoed across the canyon, then a third.

He lit the fire in the doorway, blowing gently on the flame, then hurried back to the edge of the cliff. He had to move slowly and carefully backwards down the slick steps carved into the rock, feeling his way along in the dark.

Two more shots exploded through the canyon in quick succession. Relic reached level ground and ran as fast as he could past his hidden pack and toward the source of the gunfire.

He crossed the open ground, heading slightly upstream and toward the creek. No more shots were firing, so he slowed his pace, not knowing when he might encounter Luke. He moved to a shadowed bush, squatted down, and listened.

In the distance, he heard the clack of metal on metal, Luke closing the bolt on his rifle, then a string of curses.

Relic pulled his slingshot from his pants pocket and felt about for a walnut-sized rock. When he had one, he fired it in a high arch to the left of where he thought Luke would be and he heard it rustle the brush when it fell.

Relic held his breath, listening again for Luke. He heard slow movement to his right, Luke's boots striking the ground in even steps. He imagined Luke holding his rifle before him, ready to fire at whatever made the noise, making his way toward the ruins.

Relic looked back toward the cliff. The flickering light of his doorway fire cast an eerie glow among the stone structures, glittering against the walls of the ancient homes, flashing across the pueblo then retreating into a subtle radiance. He could hear Luke moving in front of him, crossing between him and the creek, closing in on the sandstone wall below the ruins.

Suddenly, the fire in the window blushed a coral phosphorescence, lending a sense of life and of movement in the abandoned ruins. Then the glow burst into a harsher glare, illuminating the walls around it and the depths of the room behind. He could tell that Luke had stopped, no doubt watching the new blaze with some surprise. The foil had blown aside or been burned through by the flame, making it seem like someone was up there, still lighting fires in the ruins. It was just the effect Relic wanted.

Boots skidded across the ground more quickly now, Luke marching to the base of the cliffs. Luke scanned his light ahead of him then turned it off. He couldn't climb the sandstone and hold his lantern at the same time.

Stars filled the blackened sky with glowing dots

a million light years away, but the moon had still not risen, leaving the ground in deep shadows. Relic crossed the flats by memory, careful to listen for any change in Luke's direction or pace. Relic heard Luke brush along the stone until he found the shallow stairs and began to climb.

When Relic reached the bottom of the carved steps, he could hear Luke ahead and above him and figured he was about halfway to the top. He knew Luke could not fire at him while he was balanced on the slick indentations, so Relic pulled out his slingshot again and felt along the base of the cliff for a handful of rocks. He pulled back the sling, aimed in the dark, and let the first stone fly.

Luke released a grunt of surprise as the projectile struck its mark. Relic pulled and released the slingshot as quickly as he could, firing rock after rock up the slope, hearing them strike soft tissue again and again.

Luke lost his footing and screamed.

Like the sound of marbles in a tumbler, Luke rolled down the cliff, his rifle clacking against the stone, then his body sliding downward, then his rifle banging again, then his body, until he struck the ground with a resounding thump.

CHAPTER 44

Owen sucked a deep breath of air, quieting his thoughts, smoothing the jitters and spasms in his neck and back. He was free of Luke's torment, and he had to concentrate on the here and now, on what to do next. He rubbed the palms of his hands on his hips, feeling the reassurance of it, and took another breath of the cool night sky.

He and Suzy saw a lone flame light the walls of the ruins above them, across the creek, and stared at it. Faint sounds of movement reached them from the cliff and they strained to hear more. Then a second flame appeared in an upper window, the two lights glowing like a pair of uneven cat eyes in the dark, waking the fortress from its past, casting them and the historic pueblo into an identical moment in time.

"What the hell." Owen shifted his feet.

"That can't be Luke…" Suzy said.

"No, you're right. It must be Relic. But why…" Owen heard the sounds of students behind them, calling to each other to see the lights in the ruins. "That's it. It's the distraction Relic talked about before. He's keeping Luke busy for a while, so we can get to Angela, figure a way out of here."

"Right. Let's go find her." Suzy turned on a flashlight and aimed it at the ground, searching for a trail. Behind them, students milled about their tents, beams crossing each other, words floating across the distance.

Night had draped its heavy shadow on everything below the horizon. Owen could see nothing except what arose under the focus of someone's lantern.

Suzy's flashlight found a spot of flattened grass, and she followed it to a light trail leading toward the camp. Owen followed as she moved carefully along. In a few minutes, they were within speaking range of some of the students and Suzy called out for Angela. Someone answered, "Not here," another said, "Over there," her light pointing farther up the trail toward the big tent used by Everett, Luke, and Johnson. They worked their way past the others, who stood staring at the ancient ruins across the creek, speculating about the lights, joking about the spirits of Ghost Creek.

"Angela!" Suzy moved closer to one of the student's tents.

"Suzy?"

"Over here."

Suzy shined the light on her own face, so Angela could find her. Another flashlight approached.

"Suzy, I see you," Angela said.

"Hey, Angela, we've got to talk." They moved closer to each other.

"Of course, Suzy, what is it? Who's with you?"

They met on the trail and stopped.

"Remember Owen?" Suzy shined the light in his face for a moment and he blinked.

"Uh…with the pilot?"

"Yes," Owen nodded.

"Is that your work?" Angela pointed to the lights in the ruins.

"Sort of."

"We need to go somewhere private." Suzy looked around.

"The big tent's empty." Angela pointed her light up the trail and started in that direction. "Come along."

Suzy nodded an assurance to Owen and motioned him to follow her. The three walked a few minutes in silence and reached the large, canvas tent. No lights shone from inside and Owen could see none in the vicinity. Angela focused her light on the tent flap, pushed it aside, and entered.

Suzy and Owen slid into the tent as Angela lit a propane lantern, its metallic hiss rising at first, then dimming to a dull hum. Angela set it on a table in the middle of the tent, illuminating the space around them and the dark blue sides of the shelter. She turned off her flashlight and set it on the table. Suzy turned her light off, too, and they all turned to face each other.

"What's going on?" Angela asked. "There are lights in the old ruins and the students are wandering around in the dark. Everyone's agitated, and I haven't seen Everett or the other guys. And now, well…no offense to you," she motioned toward Owen, "but what the hell are you doing here? Didn't you and that nice pilot friend of yours fly out of here a couple of days ago?"

Owen told Angela what had happened after they'd flown away from the camp: that Luke had shot Thomas; that he'd brought the plane down in the river; that he'd escaped up a side-canyon; that he'd made his way back to camp to warn her and the students. Angela's eyes widened with each part of the tale. He left out any mention of Relic and Suzy gave him a curious look, but said nothing.

"Luke shot and killed Thomas?"

"There's more…" Suzy turned to Angela. "Luke tied Owen against a tree along the creek, walked away, and then used him for target practice."

Angela's skin turned ashen.

"Damn near killed him."

"Suzy heard me, I guess. She cut me loose and we've just now come up the trail to find you."

"Jesus, Suzy," Angela held her hand to her brow.

"We have to gather up the students and get the hell out of here." Suzy's voice raised an octave.

"We have to take the truck and load everyone up," Owen added, scooping his hand through the air. "Before Luke comes back into camp."

"I think you have more than Luke to worry about." The sudden sound of Everett's voice chilled the interior. Owen's muscles tensed, locked into place as Everett moved from behind them to the opposite side of the table, pistol aimed at Owen's stomach.

CHAPTER 45

He noticed a look pass quickly between Angela and Everett, and he wondered what it was about. She'd probably trusted him, worked alongside him at the site for weeks and now, this, a gun pointed at them, the threat vibrating deep in his voice, the boyish smile gone, menace in his eyes.

They stared at each other for a moment and Angela slid closer to Suzy, away from Everett. Her movement seemed to intrigue Everett, who let a tiny grin lift his right lip before dropping it back down.

The unknowns, the hidden purposes, the uncertainty of it all swirled through Owen's mind and made his head ache. He'd been shot out of the sky, chased, turned into an object of sport, prey without defense, all for what? Relic said he'd seen the three stooges, as he'd called them, carrying boxes of something to the archeological dig, moving about with them, taking things in and out of them, then returning uneventfully to their tents…

"Just what the hell are you people doing here?" Owen's hands clenched into fists. "What's that body doing behind the hangar, out there in the dirt?"

Everett's left brow rose.

"What could be so damned important to you that you'd hide a body, shoot a pilot out of the air, and come after me like I was a piece of meat?" Owen felt the blood flush through his cheeks.

Suzy waved her hand toward the boxes in the tent. "Hey, I think I know…"

Everett looked at her.

"These boxes you bring to the dig site each day, they're filled with artifacts, aren't they? You're bringing artifacts out to the site then back here for something…"

Everett grinned and stepped back. "You're right…"

Suzy's eyes were filled with worry. She moved closer to Angela.

Owen folded his arms across his chest.

"Black market, you'd probably call it." Everett relaxed his arm, lowering the pistol a couple of inches. "It's all about the provenance, you know." Everett looked at Angela and waited a moment. Turning back to Suzy, he explained, "the artifacts are gathered from museums and private collections locally, here in the state."

"Stolen, you mean," Suzy nearly whispered.

"Yes," Everett glared at her for a moment. "Then, we bring them here to the dig site, lay them into the dirt, and take measurements and photographs. I personally fill out the logs, showing each artifact unearthed right here, at the soon to be famous Ghost Creek site."

"What?" Owen dropped his hands to his side. "That works?"

"Sure. All we need is to have some form of proof where the artifacts are found, some documentation. See…" Everett glanced at Angela again, "artifacts on the black market are one thing, one kind of price point. But artifacts with colorable forms of provenance, something that looks genuine, increases the value tenfold. Buyers don't want to have to hide their collections or worry about being busted. We sell them not only interesting pieces for their collections, most of them on the east coast, but also documents showing that their artifact was found on private property, fully legal. In fact, the find has been verified by the university, by the field officer teaching the course, with a simple pen, a forgery here and there, and some university letterhead." Everett smiled.

"Forgery?" Owen asked.

"How do you think we got a written contract from the owner – her permission to dig here? I've met the old woman. She'll never know she *didn't* sign… If I say so myself," he glanced at Suzy, "I've got the gift for it."

"But sooner or later, the police will figure it out." Owen said it without much conviction.

"Not likely."

"But the pieces will be marked, logged and photographed by each of the museums. It's not hard to show they were stolen," Suzy said.

"Identifying marks, like numbers made in ink, are removed. The police would have to compare photographs from the museum with the real thing, and with photos we take here, showing where they were uncovered. But they won't have our photos, only our buyers will. And even if an artifact can be shown to be stolen, the new owner is free and clear – no criminal intent. He bought it from a dealer who sold it on behalf of the owner of lands here at Ghost Creek, a find verified by the university. And of course we, and the dealer, are long gone. At most, the final customer might lose the piece, but even that's not likely in all the confusion."

Shit. Owen looked to the ground, searching for a flaw in their grand scheme. Suzy moved her hand to her pants, and Owen noticed as she pulled a small stun gun from her pocket and slid it into Angela's hand. The two women looked at each other, and Angela stepped away from Suzy, closer to Everett's side. Owen decided to keep Everett talking.

"You still haven't told us: what about the body I found in the dirt back there?" Owen pointed to the rear of the tent, toward the shallow grave behind the hangar.

Angela inched closer to Everett.

"That? We've buried them deeper now, an unfortunate end to a juvenile delinquency…" Everett looked up, searching for words. "A simpleton tart and her lovestruck boyfriend. Neither could be trusted, ironically, in part because they brought us the most valuable pieces of all, the only pieces that actually might be traced back to the museum." He looked back at Owen. "And they wanted more money than we had on hand. Like anyone else," he drew out his words and smiled, "we're on a budget."

Suzy took a small step away from Angela, toward Owen.

"And the mastermind, if you will…"

"That's enough." Angela moved around the edge of the table and set the small stun gun next to the lantern.

Everett pointed to Angela and smiled.

CHAPTER 46

Relic turned on his penlight and shined it toward where Luke had fallen. He had to move closer before he was sure that the lump on the ground was human. He hurried to Luke's side and felt his neck for a pulse.

The man was still alive.

Relic untangled the ammunition sling from Luke's shoulders and pulled it away. Bullets were jammed into the sling in singular, open-ended pockets of cloth, one bullet per pocket, all lined against each other like a tight row of corn. He reached for the rifle, a nice looking 30.06, then stopped. That gun had likely been used to kill the girl Owen found half-buried behind the Quonset hut and it had killed Thomas, Owen's pilot friend, for sure. He did not want his fingerprints all over a murder weapon. He'd already grabbed the ammo sling, so he draped it over his head and shoulder.

A rifle with no ammunition would be useless to Luke.

His pack and the rope he needed to tie up Luke were back at some rocks by the base of the cliff. He stood to retrieve what he needed when a voice called out from the creek.

"Is anybody out here? Are you OK?"

Relic turned off his flashlight and watched as another light scanned the ground and moved toward him.

"Hello?"

It was a young woman's voice, one he didn't recognize.

He turned his light back on and walked toward her. "Are you one of the students here?"

She stopped. "Yes."

"I'm a friend of Owen's, the Park Service guy who was here a couple of days ago. He flew in and landed near the hangar."

"Oh, yes, I remember him."

Relic moved to within a few feet of her and shined the light on his own face. He smiled.

"I don't know you…" she said, some fear in her voice.

"No, but you know that guy over there," Relic shined the light toward Luke. "The guy with the rifle, who patrols here."

"Yeah, I heard gunshots. He's always shooting at targets. It makes me nervous."

"Well, that guy makes me nervous, too, and the shots you heard were him..."

"Wait, why is he...?" She hopped back a step. "Oh, oh, oh, oh." Her flashlight shined on Luke's back. "He's dead!"

"No."

"Dead. A dead body!" She backed another step.

"No. Luke is knocked out, but maybe not for long. You should get to your fellow students and warn them, right away."

"I don't know..." She shifted her weight from one foot to the other.

"We've got to help Suzy and Owen, right now, and get everyone out of here. The men in the tents, by the hangar, are dangerous. Luke shot someone out behind the hangar a few days ago. We are trying to get all the students out of here."

"What?"

"Listen, we don't have a lot of time."

"Oh god, oh god, no..." Her voice quivered. She raised her hands to her face, the light from her lantern aimed into the night sky.

"It's OK, we just have to go warn them."

"Heeeelp!" she screamed, her feet rising and falling, running in place.

Relic moved quickly to her side and took her free hand. He pulled gently forward, stretched to arm's length, and kept his eyes on hers. "It's OK, it's OK…"

She stopped her scream and gasped for air.

"Let's go get the other students…" Relic tugged her arm and moved her steadily toward the little creek. As they splashed across, he let go of her hand and she began to fall behind. He angled his way toward the big tents in the distance.

CHAPTER 47

"You…you're working with them?" Suzy's face reddened.

"Angela's the one who planned the whole thing," Everett spoke with pride in his voice. "My girl." He put his hand around her waist.

Angela smiled at him and turned back to Suzy and Owen.

"You're a professor at the college – why would you do this?" She stood with Owen.

"I should be a full, tenured professor by now, but, no, the department chair has passed me over four times and I'm tired of it. You see, Suzy, I've got the credentials but no professorship, no tenure, no authority. They treat me like a lackey, doing all the hard work, all the real work, out in the field. I got sick of it all." She flipped her blonde braid over her shoulder.

"She's brilliant, really," Everett waved the pistol toward her. "Planned it all out from the beginning. Get consent from the owner for the dig, approval from the college, a bunch of students out here – the college credit is legitimate – and there you have it!" He slipped his hand from her waist and stretched his arms. "All the best artifacts from museums across the whole area, re-discovered at the Ghost Creek site, right here, on private property. College agrees the owner keeps whatever is found, so long as it's properly photographed and recorded. That creates the perfect provenance, documented by the college itself. The land owner – through us, of course – sells what is found to private collectors. It's nearly ten times what we could get if we sold these without any proof of ownership."

"Some kind of reverse archeological looting – instead of stealing artifacts from the site, you're stealing from the museums and bringing the artifacts to the site." Suzy shook her head.

"Fucking brilliant." Everett smiled broadly at Angela, who actually blushed.

"But now we know about it," Owen whispered. Suzy leaned closer to him, her eyes tense with worry.

"Yes," Angela began.

"Hey, is Everett in there?" A graveled voice floated

from afar and through the canvas wall.

Owen turned toward the sound.

"Luke's been hurt… I've got him here, but he's unconscious. Can you help us?"

"Shit." Everett stamped his foot on the ground. A flashlight swirled around the outside of the tent, casting quick shadows across his face.

Angela patted the air with her hands, telling Everett to stay still. "Coming!" She walked behind Everett and toward the tent flaps. She stopped to take a breath, then slid quickly outside, closing the canvas flap behind her.

Everett moved back a step from the table, his eyes watching the motion of light outside. They heard another plea for help, "Over here," or something similar, and could sense that Angela had moved farther away from the tent.

They stood there in silence, watching each other, glancing at the entrance. Luke was hurt, but someone was helping him. Owen no longer saw any light from outside and realized that their own forms must be visible as silhouettes, backlit by the humming propane lantern. Whoever was out there could see them.

CHAPTER 48

Everett took two steps toward the tent flap, listening intently. Owen moved slowly behind Suzy.

Suzy stared at the ground for a moment, thinking, then looked up at Everett. "So…" she shifted to face him more directly. "You and Angela, I would never have figured the two of you together. She's beautiful, that Angela. She could have any man she wanted."

Everett continued to listen at the tent entrance. They could hear muted voices and boots shuffling across the ground, but not much else.

Owen stepped farther away from Suzy and Everett.

"Angela's a real flirt, too," Suzy tried to put a hint of female pride in her voice. "She's hit on several of the boys here on the dig, you know."

"Shut up." Everett glanced at them, then back toward the entrance.

"Bruce. She had some kind of fling with Bruce, you know him?" Suzy opened her hands toward Everett. "Everyone in camp heard about it, you know…"

Owen slid slowly along the side of the table farthest from Everett.

"She bragged about it, even…"

Everett turned to her, snarling. "Bullshit. I know what you're trying to do." He pointed the revolver at her stomach. "Now shut up."

Owen froze. Everett turned back to the entrance and moved a half step closer to it, leaning forward, listening for some sign. He held his pistol toward Suzy, but it drifted away from her as he stared at the tent flap.

Owen began to move up the table on the other side now, across from Suzy and toward the lantern. They all remained silent, straining to hear something, anything, from outside that told them what the hell was going on. Owen reached slowly for the small stun gun on the table. Suzy saw him and her brown eyes widened like glass marbles, her lips tight, her fingers balled into fists.

"Who the hell?" Angela's voice cut through the distance.

Everett leaned a little closer to the entrance.

Owen flicked on the switch and a crackle of light

flashed as he lunged forward.

Everett turned his body toward Owen and raised his pistol when the stun gun jarred into Everett's stomach and his face twisted, his eyes rolled back into his head, his fingers, outstretched starfish, dropped the gun, a desperate tension shaking through the muscles in his neck and chest as he slumped to the dirt.

CHAPTER 49

Suzy leapt for the fallen pistol and felt her left ankle pop but she grabbed the gun and aimed it at Everett, who moaned and twisted on the ground. She had him under control.

"Hey, I think I know that voice outside, earlier. I should go check." Owen stepped over Everett and ran from the tent. He stumbled, but kept moving toward a mixture of lights and sounds, about thirty yards away, until he stood at the edge of the excitement.

There stood Relic, leaning over Angela's form, his arms folded, his expression unreadable. Owen clucked his tongue and walked up to him.

"Wow." He looked down at Angela. "Thanks."

"Not used to hitting a lady…" Relic mused. He shined his penlight at her face.

"How did you know…?"

"I heard your voice so I came up close, outside the tent. I heard enough to know this woman is working with the thieves."

"We've got Everett now." Owen turned the stun gun in his hand, examining it more closely.

"Now maybe we can get back to getting these students out of here."

"Yes." Owen stuffed the stun gun into his rear pocket. He sighed and stared out across the canyon. "Fire in the ruins – that was your idea?"

"Yep."

Owen nodded. Two pinpricks of light still flickered in the dark stone structures, past lives home for the evening meal. "Where's Luke?"

"Out cold, at the base of the cliffs. For now."

The night sky had lightened, ever so subtly, in the east, smaller stars fleeing from the onset of morning. Shadows began to split apart, attach to taller objects, and reach across the plain. The night had gone by quickly, but not without a cost. Owen took a deep breath of cool air, hoping it would revive him.

"Better see if Suzy can find some rope, or duct tape, something to tie up Angela and Everett."

"Right." Owen watched as several students

began to congregate nearby, casting suspicious glances at him and Relic. He went quickly back into the large tent, where Suzy was restraining Everett's hands behind his back with copious amounts of clear plastic shipping tape.

"How about that..." Owen put his hands on his hips and smiled.

Suzy looked up at him, dark curls hanging across her face. She stood and pulled her hair behind her, tucking it under her collar, and looked back at her handiwork. Everett's mouth was taped shut.

"He's not going to be making any sales pitches for a while, is he?" Owen grinned. "Relic has Angela, but needs the tape when you're done. If there's any left..."

"Smartass." She smiled and went about wrapping more tape on Everett, first around one ankle, then the next, then both together. She tore off the roll and handed it to Owen.

The pistol lay on the table-top, under the light of the lantern. "What about that?" Owen pointed to it. "Take it with us?"

"I don't know...maybe just take the bullets out?"

Owen nodded. He pushed out the spindle, emptied each of the bullets into his hand, then slid them into his pocket.

"Those things make me nervous." She waved her palm toward the gun.

"Here," Owen set down the pistol and pulled the stun gun from his pocket. "I think this is yours."

"Well, this is different." She limped forward and reached for the slender device. "It was Angela's, but I kinda like it."

"Hurt your foot?" Owen pointed.

"Ankle. It'll be OK."

"We gotta get everyone moving out of here."

"Agreed." She put her hands on her hips. "Where's Luke?"

"Relic says he's out cold, but that may not last much longer."

"And, isn't that Johnson guy coming back today, for another load of artifacts?"

"Shit, I'd forgotten about him."

"We need to find some proof about what they've been doing here." She raised the lantern and moved around the large tent with it. A row of boxes anchored the canvas toward the back. "Here, help me with these."

Suzy set the lantern on the ground, and she and Owen moved the boxes onto the table, twelve in all. She set the lantern on one and opened the box next to it. Inside was a file folder on top of crinkled newspaper, used as packing material. The folder had several documents, one with the college letterhead. She read the memo quickly and glanced at the pictures.

"What?" Owen raised the lantern.

"Just like Everett said. The box has several artifacts in it, each with a letter of authenticity from the college, signed by the professor for this course…"

"Angela."

Suzy nodded. "And photos showing the find in situ – where it was supposedly discovered, here, in the ground, at Ghost Creek."

"These must be the product, if you will. The items being sold to collectors."

"Terrible. What a terrible scam," she shook her head.

Owen watched Everett squirm on the ground. They're stealing history, robbing a culture, cheating all of us, he thought. Especially the Pueblo people.

"Lay still or I'll add more tape to your mouth," Suzy barked at Everett, and he obeyed.

"This box looks heavy," Owen pointed, "and it has a star drawn on it."

Suzy stepped gingerly to the cardboard flaps and tore them open. Inside, two small, three-ring binders stood upright against an expandable file folder and a ledger notebook. She pulled out the ledger and moved closer to the lantern.

"Yes, yes, this is it!"

"What?"

"Names of museums, lists of items stolen, correlating the item with the new work-up, the stuff to be sold. Sale prices listed, too."

"A Rosetta stone, of sorts."

"Yes." She looked up at him, her eyes alight. "This will let us track every single item back to its museum." She slipped the thin ledger behind her back, under her belt.

A wrapped cloth fit snugly in the back of the box. She pulled it out, set it on the table, and carefully unwound it. Four sleeves were sewn into the cloth, each holding separate objects. She pulled the first one partway out and examined it.

"Whoa, this is beautiful…"

The sound of unhappy voices rose outside the tent.

"We gotta go," Owen motioned to the exit.

Suzy slid the figurine back into its sleeve.

CHAPTER 50

Outside, shadows thinned against the warming sky and the slow simmer of waking students began to boil. Owen followed Suzy as she limped to Relic with the roll of packing tape. Angela still lay at his feet, unconscious. Relic maneuvered her arms behind her back and Owen began wrapping her wrists.

"I'll get my friend Victor to drive," Suzy yelled as she moved into the gathering students.

"Hey!" Bruce objected. He stepped forward from the crowd.

"It's OK," Owen stepped toward him. "Turns out, Angela's working with Everett and the others. Luke is still out there," he pointed into the darkness of the cliffs across the creek, "and Johnson is coming back. We've got to get the hell out of here."

"How do we know you're not in it with Everett,

and you're not tying up Angela to protect yourself?" Bruce looked at Relic. "And who the hell are you, anyway? For all we know, you're the one looting artifacts…" He put his hands on his hips.

Relic spoke to Owen: "Find the keys to the truck and get these folks into it."

Owen stepped away and began talking to the other students, explaining how he worked with the Park Service, that Suzy could verify that they all needed to hop into the long-bed truck. "No time for your gear, just get in now," he urged.

Bruce stepped closer to Relic. "We're not taking orders from you."

Owen turned back toward Bruce and Relic.

Relic touched the handle of his hunting knife and pulled it partway from its sheath.

Bruce stared at the pointed shape, then looked into the unyielding eyes of the wild-looking man with the knife on his belt.

"Uh, sure, I get it…get in the truck and get the hell out of here. Couldn't pay me not to." Bruce turned and moved quickly toward the pickup truck.

Owen looked to Relic, then glanced at the knife, his question implicit.

Relic smiled sheepishly and shrugged. "No

patience for jackasses…" He pushed the blade back into its sheath.

Owen nodded.

"Help me get Angela into one of these tents." Relic reached under her armpits and lifted, careful to keep her head pitched onto her chest. Owen hurried to carry her feet and they stumbled with her to a nearby tent, where Relic ducked inside and pulled her in after him. He slid back out and zipped it shut.

"Why in the tent?" Owen brushed off his pants.

"She's still out of it. The tent will hide her from Luke for a while, if he comes around…"

"Got it."

"Next is a bit tricky…" Relic moved toward Owen. "Explain to the driver…" he pointed to the truck "…he has to drive on the old ruts, to the right of the hill and wait. It might take a while, or it might be right away, but he'll see the dust from Johnson's truck as Johnson comes down the main dirt road."

Owen nodded.

"All the students have to stay in the truck and keep their voices down…"

"Easier said than done."

"Just the same… Then, when they see the dust go round, behind the hill, the students have to drive farther on the old two-track. They go on the right side of the hill while Johnson goes left, on the good road. They have to sneak past him, essentially. When he's on the left, they go on the right to reach the better road, then go as fast as they dare all the way to the sheriff."

"Got it."

"So, Owen," Relic slowed his speech and grinned. "I gotta ask – you still tempted to take me in?" He offered his wrists in mock surrender.

"Shit, Relic, give me a break. You could've run off on me miles ago, and being a lawman, well, that's just not in my nature. But watch yourself – there's a reward out for you now."

Relic's eyes widened. "How much?"

"Ten grand."

"That all?" he sniffled.

Owen reached for Relic's hand and they shook, then patted each other on the back.

"I gotta get back to my still…"

"How am I going to explain you, I mean, what you've done here?"

Relic stroked his goatee. "Well…Luke never saw me coming…"

"But Suzy, and some of the other students…"

"Maybe no one knows who I was. Just some hiker

they remember, sort of, gift-wrapping Angela."

"Maybe we'll remember that Victor did that…" Owen raised a brow.

"Confusion everywhere, no one fully sure what they saw that night…" Relic gazed at Owen from under his hat, testing his theory.

"Sounds about right to me."

"I owe you one."

Owen was pretty sure Relic had it backwards for once. "I'll see if Victor's driving, and I'll explain the plan to him, about waiting for Johnson to go round the hill before he drives them out of here."

Suzy's voice reached them. "I've found the keys."

Boots shuffled across the hard ground as students carried laptops, clothes, notebooks, and daypacks with them into the truck. One still held onto his can of Budweiser. So much for being quick.

"Everyone, pile in the front and in the bed of the truck. Hurry now." Suzy handed the keys to Victor, who sat behind the wheel of the truck. She began waving people into the back, pointing at each student and counting out loud as she did. "I got twenty-two, not counting me." Four students sat with their backs against each of the side walls of the truck bed. Four more sat with their backs to the cab and another four at the tailgate, knees pulled to their chests. Three students crammed into the middle and three more into the front seat. She waved to Owen and Relic. "It's a tight fit but that's everybody."

"Hop in and go," Owen pointed at the truck behind her.

"What's the plan for you guys?" Suzy asked.

"We'll take off, back up the creek," Relic nodded in that direction. "We'll stay a safe distance and watch 'till the sheriff shows up."

Owen hadn't really thought about it until now, but it was a decent plan. "There's no more room in the truck bed anyway, maybe just for one more, for you, in the cab."

"OK." Suzy glanced back. They heard the engine turn over and white smoke rumbled gently out of the exhaust.

"Oh, guys," Suzy turned toward them. "Check out the big blue tent before you go, the artifacts on the table. There's a beautiful figurine there, ceramic I'd say. Looks really old."

"Sure," Owen nodded.

"Meet you all back at the sheriff's office?"

"You bet," Owen smiled.

Relic glanced away.

******

Suzy turned and hobbled back to the pickup. The bed was full of warm bodies, thigh to thigh, back to back, practically one on top of the other, with no place for anyone else to sit or lay. She opened the passenger side door to the cab and there sat Bruce, grinning lasciviously.

"No…" Suzy whispered the words, more in denial than surprise.

"Sure, hon, I knew you wanted some of this." He pointed to his lap. "Hop on!" Bruce tossed his head back and laughed.

Something inside of her steamed through an over-used safety valve, suddenly and decidedly unstuck, and with one smooth motion, she removed the stun gun from her pocket, flicked the switch, and held it above Bruce's crotch. His laughter stopped in mid-air, his breath suddenly ragged. She pulled back the stun gun and slammed the door in his face.

She limped around the front of the truck and to the driver's side door.

Victor stared wide until Bruce stopped gasping then turned to Suzy, his eyes at full attention.

"Go on, I'll stay back with these guys," she pointeded toward Owen and Relic.

Victor nodded, shifted gears, and began to pull the truck away. She turned to avoid the rear tire, her left ankle buckled, and she went down to the ground with a "hummpf."

CHAPTER 51

The pickup rolled slowly away from the tents as Suzy picked herself up. When she tried to stand on her left foot, a bolt of pain shot through her ankle and up her leg and she hopped onto her right foot.

"Damn, damn, damn." She squeezed her eyes shut and rebalanced herself.

The truck moved away at a steady clip, dipping and rising with the ground as it angled toward the back of the hill.

Owen and Relic walked to her side.

"Thought I'd stay with you guys after all," she said, teetering on her good foot.

"You OK?" Owen tapped his shoulder and she accepted, laying her left hand there for balance.

"Damn."

"Let me see." Relic squatted by her ankle and took

it gently in hand. He turned it slowly left and right.

"Shit!" Her face tightened, eyes clamped shut.

"OK." Relic released her foot and stood up again. "May have sprained it." He looked at them both. "You can't run on this…"

She shook her head. "We have plenty of time, don't we? We can walk away and hide, right?" she asked.

Owen adjusted his stance to take more of her weight.

"Might have, earlier." Relic pointed behind them. "Not any more…"

Owen turned to look. "Shit."

A streak of dust hung over the plateau to the south. "That's from the dirt road, coming this way," Relic said.

"Johnson?" she asked.

"No one else." Relic looked around the camp, scanning the distant student tents, the large canvas shelter where the artifacts were packaged, the Quonset hut that anchored the tarp to the main tent. The sun had risen only slightly higher on the horizon, but flames of light now cast across the little canyon like a dozen flares, honey drizzled on boxelder leaves, amber sprayed atop the sage and grass of the open plain. His gaze returned to the hut and he stepped closer to see inside the rudimentary hangar.

"What about this?" he pointed at the old Aeronca. "You flew that other plane, the Cessna…"

Suzy hobbled with him as Owen turned toward Relic. "Damn, Relic, I flew that one right into the river!"

"So avoid a water landing this time…" Relic shrugged.

"Smartass."

"I can help," Suzy smiled.

"What?"

"My grandfather flew, taught me some…"

"You're a pilot?" Owen asked.

"No, but I can help…"

"Not with that," Owen pointed to her foot.

"I'll instruct…"

Owen looked sideways at her.

"Look, folks, we need a decision right now." Relic pointed behind them. A rooster tail of dust rose into the morning sky, signaling where Johnson's truck was barreling down the main road. The students' truck was right where it should be, hidden from Johnson, behind the hill. Soon, Johnson would pass beyond the old two-track, the intersection, such as it was, and drive onto the left side of the knoll. The students would begin their trek to the main road when they saw the dust from Johnson's truck change direction. Once that happened, Owen and Suzy had minutes to get the plane in the air or try something completely different.

CHAPTER 52

"Shit. I can't fly that antique. I can't fly anything."
Owen exhaled a long breath.

"Stop listening to that voice in your head." Relic
and Owen exchanged a serious look. Owen glanced
at the ground.

Relic was right. It wasn't his own voice he heard
in his head anymore, and that was progress, of a sort.
The sound of it had changed and now he could hear a
hint of Probation Officer Pete, telling him to stay realistic, grounded.

"I'm not running anywhere in this condition."
Suzy grabbed Owen's arm and began hopping toward the plane. "But get me in there and I'll talk you
through it."

Owen could not help but be carried along.

Relic ran to the plane and began pushing it out of

the hangar, onto the flattened grass on the south end of the old airstrip. He let it roll to a slow stop. Tendrils of worn fabric hung from the wing tips like errant hairs. A section of material had been pulled from the fuselage behind the door, revealing the metal framing underneath. A series of small patches, cut with zig-zag scissors, lay plastered across the body of the plane behind the rear window. Streaks of old, black oil ran down the metal cowling above the engine.

Suzy pulled Owen with her and they ducked and hobbled under the long, yellow wing to the passenger side. She opened the door, skipped free of Owen's grasp and slid into the seat. Gingerly, she pulled her left foot into the plane with her hands. She reclined in the seat, the thieves' ledger still under her belt, rubbing against her back.

"Hurry!" Suzy tucked her right leg in and slammed the cabin door closed. She began to maneuver the yoke forward and back, turning it left and right, watching to make sure it moved the horizontal at the tail and the ailerons on the wings.

Owen ran behind the plane and forward again to the pilot seat. The foam on the bottom had been ripped out and a thick towel lay in its place. He took a breath and hopped in.

"Seat belt," Suzy said as she tightened her own.

He latched the old-style clasp together and stared at the console. Like an antique car, the dash was made of lacquered metal, an instrument panel sparse to the point of being barren. A tube-like contraption rested in the center of the dash, just under the windshield, bobbing gently. Markings on the side told him it was the fuel gauge, half-full. The controls at least had dual yokes, one for him, one for Suzy. Flying with just a stick would have seemed even more impossible. There was an ignition, the key in place, and a knob attached to a long rod, which he figured from his flight in the Cessna was the throttle. A compass spun lazily in front of him and a needle on the air speed indicator rested on zero. He could not see any radios or navigational equipment.

"Feel the foot petals," Suzy pointed below him. He set his boots on them and pushed forward and back. "Point with your toes to brake. To steer, keep only your heels on the pedals and push."

"Which way?"

"Push right to go right, left to go left." Suzy turned, watching the tail move with the pedals.

Owen nodded. "Wait. I can't see a damned thing." The plane angled upward as it sat, its tail resting on a small wheel at the rear of the craft.

"Lean out the window."

"No shit?"

"Look left. Put the engine cowling in your peripheral view then look down runway about two hundred feet. That'll give you some depth perception and let you keep the nose of the plane on the runway."

Owen shook his head.

"Until the plane is moving fast enough, that's how you have to steer."

"No. Really?"

"Yes. Really. When the plane is moving fast enough, the rear raises up and you can see level in front of you."

"Shit," he whispered under his breath. He peered out the open window, trying for a sense of direction that would take them down the runway.

Suzy reached to another knob on his left, pulled it out, in, out, and back in again. "Primer," she said.

"Now what?"

"Relic!"

Relic moved to the front of the plane.

"Spin the prop," Suzy yelled. "Put your hands on the end and pull it through slowly two or three times. The ignition's off, so it shouldn't start yet, but be ready to step away if it does. Owen, feet on the brakes!"

Owen straightened his legs against the pedals.

Relic dropped his weight into the pull to make the propeller rotate once, then again, and a third time. The fourth time, it seemed to move more easily. He stopped and looked at Suzy through the windshield.

"OK, Owen, turn the key and pump the throttle as Relic spins the prop. Just keep pumping, once or twice each time. Don't flood it. Relic, jump back after each pull."

Relic gave her a thumbs up.

Owen turned the key, pulled the throttle all the way back, pumped it twice, and said a prayer.

CHAPTER 53

Luke rolled on his belly like an empty dory, swinging back and forth, first to one edge then the other, groaning, finally balancing on his right side. He opened his eyes into tiny slits, staring at the base of the sandstone wall, trying to recall what had happened. Then he shifted to his stomach again and lifted himself with his arms until his legs were under him and he sat.

His head felt like a swollen cantaloupe and when he closed his eyes, the melon spun on his shoulders until he thought it would split. He held his hands onto the ground until the sea sickness stopped.

He was below the pueblo ruins, he realized, north from the camp and away from everyone else. Something, someone, had peppered him with stones and he'd slipped off the shallow footholds in the dark and rolled to the bottom. The sun had been up for some time now, still morning but well past the dawn. He touched his head and felt dried blood on this left temple.

The rifle lay to his side and when he reached for it, he grinned. Using it like a crutch, he stood and leaned against the cliff.

He remembered lights in the nighttime ruins, flickering on in one building, then another. Whoever had been up there, real or spectral, was gone by now.

His red hat lay on the ground a few feet away and his ammo belt was gone, but he still had a few bullets in the gun's magazine. It was no ghost who took twenty rounds of rifle shot and knocked him to the bottom of the cliff. He walked gingerly to his cap and pulled it tightly onto his head, wondering which student he was going to use for target practice.

CHAPTER 54

"Pull!"

Relic bounced on the balls of his feet, then put his weight into the effort, spinning the propeller once around. The blade stuttered, seemed to jerk back a few inches, then stopped completely. He tried again, feeling a kind of back pressure in the engine as he pulled and then, as it passed some inner point of resistance, it rotated faster until it stopped again.

Owen looked outside of his door. The trail of dust had shifted from its northern trajectory to directly west, coming right at them. He could no longer see the student's truck and made another silent prayer, this time that the students had made it past Johnson, on the alternate route.

"Pump the throttle as the prop starts to turn." Suzy twisted to face him.

Owen waited for Relic to try again, thinking they still had time to hide, even with Suzy's sprained ankle, behind the hangar or along the little creek. But what happened when Johnson found Everett and Angela and they all found Luke and searched the campgrounds?

Relic pulled with all his weight, slipping to the ground as the propeller spun once, then made it, barely, past that hidden resistance, and spun again, then again, then stopped cold.

"Shit on a shingle." Relic picked himself up. He widened his stance, pulled, and turned away as the propeller rotated once again, then again, then the engine backfired, but the prop kept moving, faster, and faster until the engine roared and the blade became a ghostly blur, not quite solid, not quite empty space, and the plane began to roll forward. Owen pushed on the brakes and Relic trotted away, clear of the wheels and wings, waving his approval.

"Yes!" Suzy cheered.

Owen leaned out of the window to see the grass strip, trying to keep the engine on the edge of his line of sight and aim down the middle of the runway. He could see Johnson's truck barreling toward them, the lights and grille expanding rapidly.

"Full throttle!" Suzy's brow crinkled in concentration, then she turned to watch outside her window.

Owen pushed the throttle steadily inward. The engine sputtered and he backed off, pumped the throttle again, then pushed it all the way forward. The old Aeronca moved slowly down the grass strip then, gathering speed, it was soon bouncing over the ground, jarring against dips in the field, rocking the yoke, vibrating Owen's bones and teeth and fingernails, the compass spinning, the fuel gauge bobbing wildly, and just when he was sure the wooden ribs in the wings would splinter apart, the tail rose from the ground and he was level with the horizon and could see the plateau trembling a few short miles ahead of them. The yoke seemed to pull back by itself and he glanced at Suzy, who'd made the maneuver, and in a second the torture of motion abruptly ended and they floated in the air, inches off the rugged ground.

****

Relic stood near the edge of the runway and held his breath. The yellow tail rose from the ground and, seconds later, the rest of the plane lifted from the earth and all of its gangly, teenaged awkwardness smoothed into mature flight, its tail high and proud, its wings level. The engine sounded erratic now and then, an odd shifting of noise and motion, but continued on, flying them slowly higher across the open canyon.

Johnson's truck angled away from the dirt road, away from Relic and toward the floating Aeronca, as if to chase it, but the plane had the lead and was soon higher than the pickup and Johnson slowed to a stop.

Relic walked backwards quickly, toward the Quonset hut and into the shadows. He kneeled into some untrammeled grass and watched.

To his left, toward the students' camp, a single shot was fired across the canyon. He turned his eyes back to the Aeronca.

CHAPTER 55

The shot appeared to be a clean miss. The Aeronca continued to bob and float slowly higher, farther and farther from the camp. Relic knew who had fired the rifle. He touched the ammunition belt on his shoulder, hoping he had the rest of Luke's bullets.

Relic stepped out of the shade of the Quonset hut and moved quickly into the blue family-style tent, a temporary place for cover as he worked his way toward the creek.

"Ummph."

Relic turned toward the sound. Everett lay on the ground at the far corner of the tent, rolling, struggling against the wrapping tape.

"Relax there, mister, the sheriff will cut you free. Then lock you up."

Everett stopped and glared at him.

"What do we have here?" Spread across a portable table were boxes, plates, bowls, axes, arrowheads, and a wrapped cloth the size of a small pillow. He remembered what Suzy had said about something ceramic.

He examined what was out in the open, wondering where they'd all come from, where they all belonged, then reached for a terrycloth bundle and untied the sides. Hard objects separated as he spread the sewn container and discovered sleeves stitched along the sides of the artifacts. He reached inside the first pocket and pulled out an ancient, kiln-baked figure of a man, hash marks for eyes, body spotted with dots, arms etched along the sides, chips of sea shell for a belt. Then he saw a symbol of his grandfather's clan and suddenly knew exactly where the figurines belonged.

He heard a truck door slam shut outside. He carefully rewrapped the figurines in the cloth container and glanced at the remaining objects. Too much to take with him, not sure where they belonged in any event. He tucked the figurines under his arm and moved quietly to the tent flap.

Everett began grunting again. Relic ignored him, slid to the edge of the tent, and peered outside.

The Aeronca could still be heard in the distance. Johnson was not in or near his truck and Relic knew Luke was up and about, perhaps with a few more bullets.

Johnson's voice carried to him from several yards away. The students had slipped past the man, along the opposite side of the hill, but he would soon realize they'd all left the camp. Johnson could still catch them in his fancy truck.

Relic trotted low to the ground directly toward the silver double cab and arrived at the rear wheel. He pulled his hunting knife from the sheath and wiggled the tip into the tire stem, below the valve. Air began to hiss from the slit and he put his knife away. The large tire would not go flat quickly. But if Johnson followed the college kids and Relic nicked it right, the tire would flatten somewhere along the thirty-six mile dirt road to the highway, isolated from everyone.

Relic peered under the truck but did not see anyone on the other side. He figured that Johnson went toward the students' tents, close to where Everett was all taped up. The rifle shot had come from that direction, too, so they were probably freeing Everett and figuring out what to do. They would quickly decide to take Johnson's truck out of here.

Angela was probably still taped up inside the

student tent, the one he'd slid her into. The men would likely go searching and, though it might not take them long to find her, the time they used to do it would let the students get farther away.

He sprinted back across the open ground, from the truck to the corner of the Quonset hut, tripped, caught himself, and continued on. He slid behind the hangar wall and when he slowed his breathing he could hear something again, voices toward the students' tents.

He moved to the other side of the hangar then around the outer wall. From there, he climbed a fifteen foot embankment and moved away from the edge, to an area where he could not see the camp, and no one in the camp could see him. He went steadily along the ridge until he thought he was near the camp kitchen, beyond the students' tents, past where Everett and Luke and Johnson might be, and well below the tent where Angela was restrained.

Relic kneeled at the edge of the low rise and peered over. The mess tent and kitchen were directly below him and no one was in sight. He slid as quietly as he could down the loose scree and trotted to the propane burners, where he squatted low and listened.

CHAPTER 56

Owen tilted the wings a little to the left and the Aeronca aligned with the dirt road about two hundred feet below them. He tried to take a deep breath, but his chest would not allow it. Suzy squirmed next to him, groaning quietly in some measure of pain, moving her swollen ankle with her hands.

"Are we OK?" Owen asked over the sound of the engine.

"Great. Keep her wings level and pull back a bit. Get us some altitude." She took the yoke and showed him.

The plane rose slowly, the engine under greater strain.

"There." She pointed to the yoke in his hands and released her grip. He could feel some pressure on the wheel as he held it in place.

"We can follow the dirt road to the highway, then find the airport from there, if you know the general direction." Suzy tucked her swollen foot behind the other.

"I think we go left at the highway. I know it leads close to the airport," Owen nodded.

"Once we see the airstrip, we're home free."

Owen nodded again, hoping she was correct. To their right, rough-carved cliffs rose high above them. To their left, the wide river laid a swath of brown across a broken landscape, uniform and smooth, carving and curving through the gorge, a snake with the patience of eons.

He tilted the wings farther left, away from the high cliffs and over the river, and remembered the very sight in front of him when he and Thomas had flown here days ago. God, it seemed like months. The canyon twisted to their right and he turned in that direction and there lay the Cessna, its tail bent in the current and flashing in the desert sun, its wings just visible under the water, tortured backwards, a pair of broken arms. His eyes welled up when he thought of Thomas.

"Oh, shit, that's your plane, isn't it?" Suzy pointed to the Cessna then looked at Owen. "Sorry, Owen, so sorry." She put her hand on his shoulder and he released a sob and looked away.

Suzy helped him keep the Aeronca level.

Soon they were past the Cessna and tufts of cream dotted the river, whitewater rapids tumbling over rocks the size of cars.

The rough water bent to their right again and began to smooth as they turned. They'd gained maybe another hundred feet but the cliffs were still above them. Owen concentrated on centering the plane on the river, watching the dirt road on their right, when he noticed a plume of dust rising before them.

"The truck!" Suzy touched his shoulder with one hand and pointed with the other. She opened her window and waved. The students were traveling slowly along the rugged road and the sight encouraged him.

"Hey!"

"Waggle your wings," Suzy said.

"Waggle?"

"Wave at them with your wings."

"Oh, sure." Owen watched as students waved at them from the open bed of the truck. He couldn't hear them, but their motions and expressions were joyous, energetic. He tilted the wings to the left, dipping his side of the plane toward the river, then to the right, toward the moving truck, then back again. He knew it was not possible under the drone of the old engine, but he swore he could hear them cheering.

As they flew above them, they passed out of view and Owen turned toward Suzy. Her ivory smile was broad and real and when it spread all the way to her burnished eyes he knew he would never return to the crowds, or to what's-her-name, or her imperial father, or to Probation Officer Pete, and Owen's smile, loose and ungrounded, joined with hers.

CHAPTER 57

Everett rolled onto his back and stared at the inside roof of the large tent. Morning sunshine filled the space with a bluish light, and he thought he heard voices and scrapes and clunks in the distance. His hands were taped together behind his back and they began to ache from his own weight.

Who was that guy with the ponytail who'd come in and out of the tent? He'd run off with a hundred and fifty thousand dollars' worth of artifacts, damn it, and they were going to have to find him.

He pulled his legs to his chest and slipped onto his side. From there, he shifted to his stomach, gathering his legs beneath him. Slowly, carefully, he stood and balanced for a moment. He hobbled to the tent flap and slid outside. From there, he hopped and twisted forward, across the open grass, searching for Angela or

Johnson or Luke.

******

Damn it, he'd missed the shot. Luke could still hear the little airplane engine droning on, shrinking the yellow Aeronca into a tiny dot.

He re-shouldered his Winchester and hurried along a beaten path to a spot about fifty yards from the big tents. A motion to his left stopped him in his tracks and he pulled the rifle into his arms. There, a dozen feet to his side, stood Everett, his hands bound behind his back, his feet taped together, his mouth contorted behind a mass of clear packing tape.

"Holy mother…" Luke lowered his rifle and ran to him.

A look of relief came over Everett's face.

"What bastard did this to you? And how the hell do I unwind it?" Luke searched the tape around Everett's head then reached for a pocket knife and flipped it open. Everett stiffened, his eyes wide.

Luke found a corner and began to slice open the tape on the side of Everett's neck. When he had enough cut, he put away the knife and pulled it around and around Everett's head until he reached the last strip and it yanked on Everett's hair and skin.

"Shit, Luke, ow, ow, ow, slow down!"

Luke tugged the last of it free.

"Jesus," Everett gasped for breath.

"What the hell happened?" Luke tossed the used tape to the ground.

"They got the jump on me, inside the tent, and I rolled my way out here, trying to get free."

"They used a whole roll of tape on you."

"I know, I know, and they must have gotten Angela, too, but I haven't found her yet. Here," he turned and reached his hands outward, "cut me free of this…"

Luke looked across the open field, toward the grass airstrip. "Where's Johnson? Didn't I hear his truck?"

"Luke, I hate to say this, but I think Johnson helped all the students get away. I think he's helping them."

"What? Shit."

"Yeah, exactly. Like I told you before, Johnson's got some kind of side deal going with the dealer, and who knows what he's going to do to get us out of the way." Everett's lips tightened and he stared at Luke. "Now cut me the rest of the way loose."

"Funny you should say that," Johnson

stepped from behind a thick saltbush near an empty student tent.

Luke straightened and lifted the Winchester.

"Everett said the same thing about you, Luke," Johnson continued, "that I ought to take you out and shoot you like a coyote and, if I did, I could have your share of the split." Johnson raised his arms in the air.

Everett plopped into the dirt and squirmed, sliding his hands under his rear end. He tucked his knees into his chest and worked his bound hands past his feet, so they were no longer behind his back. He began yanking on the tape at his ankles.

"Luke, you know me," Johnson smiled. "I ain't that kinda guy. And if I was, I'da shot the both of you from behind."

Everett managed to loosen the tape on his feet. Balancing carefully, he stood up. "Shoot him, Luke, shoot him while you've got the drop on him."

"You know," Luke lowered his rifle a bit, "Johnson's got a point."

"What point, Luke?" Everett hobbled forward, pressing his face closer to Luke.

"He could've shot us both, asked questions later."

Johnson relaxed and folded his arms.

"And you told me I could have his share of the

split," Luke pointed at Johnson, "if I shot him. Funny you would make the same offer to the both of us."

Everett twisted his head toward Johnson, then Luke, then back again, his mouth open, his arms raised. "Luke, this is your chance, but you've gotta shoot him, shoot him now!"

Luke lowered his rifle and smiled at Johnson, who smiled back.

"Aw, shit, no." Everett kept his arms up, as if to block any movement from the two men.

"You're such a self-absorbed little shithead," Johnson said, adjusting his cowboy hat. "Nobody's ever as smart as you, are they, Everett? And nobody's ever worth more than you, are they?" He took a step toward him.

"We're not stupid, ass-wipe." Luke raised his rifle at Everett.

"Luke, you know you trust me," Everett took a short hop toward him, "or you wouldn't be cutting me free. Deep down, Luke, you know I would never cross you…"

"I cut your mouth free just to see what you'd say…" he raised the gun to Everett's chest.

"No, no, no," Everett knelt on the ground again, his hands still taped together, begging.

"I'll grab the cash box," Johnson said.

"And those figurines…"

"Right." Johnson strode toward the large blue tent.

"I'll make sure the ass-wipe doesn't move."

CHAPTER 58

Angela woke to a pounding headache and the inability to scratch her nose. She remembered the night before, being called out of the big tent and into the night, but not much else. She rolled over and stared at the inside top of a beige tent, one provided by the college for the students. Damn, she'd been hit from behind, rolled up like a burrito, and tossed into the nylon shelter to bake.

She struggled against the restraints without luck, but her mouth was not taped so she took a deep breath. She sat up and scooted to the edge of the tent and found it zippered shut. She turned so that her hands could reach the zipper and pulled it partway open.

She spun to face the entrance and poked her head into the morning air. Raising her head against the door-way, she slowly pushed through and rolled herself out of the little tent.

Angela's hands were tied behind her, so she pulled her knees to her chest, scooted her arms under her rear, and worked her arms around her feet, leaving her hands in front of her. She then began to unravel the tape on her feet and, although her hands were still bound, she was able to stand and kick the last of her leg restraints to the ground.

She stopped and listened. Where was everyone? To her right, fifty yards away, she could see the family-style tents she and Everett used to prepare the artifacts. To her left, more student tents spread haphazardly across the flats, but they looked abandoned. Behind and to her left were the outhouses and she could see the top of the tarp used to shade the camp kitchen a hundred yards away, closer to the little creek. Male voices carried from the other direction, at a dip in the landscape toward the dirt road. One of them sounded like Everett.

She walked toward a large saltbush and a student tent on the edge of a shallow drop. Johnson stepped into view, his back toward her, making his way toward the road and what looked like the top of his silver pickup. He went in that direction for a bit, then turned to his right and went into the large tent where they kept the catalogues and records. And cash.

Angela lowered herself and stepped closer to the

brush. She could hear scuffling of some kind in the dirt, but the voices were silent. She peered over the top of the bush and saw Luke, standing maybe ten yards away, his rifle aimed loosely at something she couldn't see. Then she heard Everett's voice.

"Don't do this, Luke, don't do it. We're a team here. If we break up we're all doomed."

"Shut up."

"We can all still get away but we've got to hurry. Grab the cash box, that's a good plan, Luke, but we can still take the artifacts, too, meet one last time with the dealer's people, south of Salt Lake. Listen to me, Luke, we can make one last score before we have to go our separate ways, and it'll be a big one."

"I said…" Luke raised the rifle to Everett's head.

"No!" Angela leapt from the bush and waved her taped-up hands in the air, charging down on Luke.

Startled, Luke spun and fired into the air.

Angela skidded to a stop in the dust, her pale eyes wide, her mouth an outstretched O-ring, her expression locked in place. Then she looked to her feet and blinked.

Luke chambered another bullet.

Angela turned and fled back up the short rise and across the open flats, her legs pounding into the dirt, knowing the next shot could kill her, knowing her only hope was to shelter behind the fiberglass build-ings in front of her, the row of outhouses above the camp kitchen.

Luke aimed a bit too quickly and the shot spun through the air just above her head. The concussion blew past her like a break in the sound barrier, shaking her bones, shoving her forward, her legs still pumping, her lungs still burning.

"Damn!" Luke tried to chamber another round.

She crossed the open flats, crashed against the side of the portable outhouse, and threw herself on the ground behind it, scooting and twisting behind the edge of the fiberglass.

CHAPTER 59

Relic pulled open the storage bin door and rummaged through. He found two large boxes of rice, cilantro lime and creamy cheese, and stacked them on the table. Next to them, he laid the figurines, still in their cushioned holder, and turned back to the kitchen supplies. Didn't they have any jerky or M&M's?

He estimated the space he'd have available in his pack, which still rested behind some rocks at the base of the cliff ruins. He didn't have room for much more, but he grabbed a stash of breakfast bars from atop a row of…canned milk? Yuck. He spied some canned meats and just as he reached for one, the sound of rifle fire flashed through the canyon.

Crack!

The sound shook the kitchen canopy over his head and a quick spasm in his back tensed and released.

He pulled his arms to his sides. He could live without the spam.

Motion in his periphery made him turn his head and he saw Angela dashing, her arms spinning, running frantically across an open expanse toward the outhouses behind the kitchen. Was she being shot at? Was the rifleman giving her cover so she could get closer to him?

Relic ducked below the propane stove and thought. Act fast, get out of here fast. Another rifle shot shocked the air and he heard Angela crash into the side of one of the outhouses. Had Luke found more ammunition? Was Everett freed from the packing tape and armed? He touched the shoulder belt he'd taken from Luke and had an idea.

He moved to the propane tanks and turned the valves full open, then twisted the dials on the stove until the hiss was steady and clear. He reached for his pocket matches, lit one, and tossed it onto the metal grill. All four burners sneezed into flame, the sound erupting like a blast of air slamming a canvas sail.

Relic slid the ammunition belt off his shoulder and rose to his feet. He spoke a count-down, one, two, three, then tossed the bullet-filled sling onto the burners, grabbed the figurines and food from the table, and ran toward Ghost Creek as fast as he'd ever moved.

CHAPTER 60

Angela peered across the flats to the spot where Luke and Everett were, then scanned for signs of any other movement. Johnson appeared to the right of the other men, carrying something heavy toward his pickup, the cash box, she realized. When he'd placed it in the bed of the truck, he called out to Luke, waving him over. Luke walked slowly backwards, looking at what Angela assumed was Everett, probably still on the ground, just out of sight. Then Luke trotted toward the truck.

Had Everett done something to make Luke and Johnson break from the team? Was Everett all right? Had Owen and the students run away?

Everett, with his rounded spectacles and slender hands, could copy any signature and she'd even seen him forge a postmark once. She didn't expect loyalty as a lover, but he was always discrete, a conniving man but a puppy, not a wolf. Luke and his errant scarecrow were lonely and weird, willing to eliminate enemies, but he was controllable. Despite the broad-brimmed hat, Johnson was no cowboy but he was biddable and dependable and had valuable local contacts, like the delinquents who'd brought them the clay figurines. So who was pissed off at whom? And why?

Angela was fully in charge of this operation and the men had all been in their proper roles, efficient, relaxed, obedient. Until now. She had to figure out what had changed and chart her next move. She had to get the hell out of this canyon with the artifacts in tow because she was never again returning to that thankless job in that backwater college town.

She moved her hand along the ground, through a sticky muck, and the smell of the outhouse assaulted her sinuses. She looked down at coffee colored goop oozing through her fingers and yelped.

"Damn it all!" She flung the loose sludge from her hand, moved away from the outhouse, and wiped her fingers in the dry dust.

"Damn it to hell!" She stood up quickly and searched for a better way to clean her hand. Several yards away, Everett hobbled into view, pleading, it seemed, as he approached Johnson and Luke, who were still at the truck.

A shot exploded from the kitchen area, on the other side of the outhouses, and Angela dropped her knees into the soupy sewage.

******

Luke and Johnson flinched at the sound of gunfire and ran behind the pickup. Another *crack* exploded from the outdoor kitchen and they ducked below the truck bed.

Crack, crack, crack, crack, four more shots, one on top of the other, rang out across the canyon, clunking into outhouse walls, zinging across the desert, slicing through nylon tents.

"Shit, who is that? How many of them are there?" Luke turned his cap on backwards and glanced over the edge of the truck.

"Use your rifle! Fire back at them!" Johnson yelled.

Luke lifted his Winchester and shrugged. "Outta ammo."

"Shit, let's get out of here." Johnson braced himself then ran to the front of the truck and slid quickly into the driver's seat.

Luke opened the passenger door and hopped inside. "Got the cash?"

"In the truck bed."

"Figurines?"

"Couldn't find 'em."

"Damn it."

Johnson started the pickup and jammed it into drive. Gravel spun from the wheels as Johnson powered forward and onto the dirt road. He and Luke kept their heads as low as they could, glancing behind them, bouncing over the washboard road like speed was their only friend in life.

****

Relic reached the trees and slid into the grass as the first shot fired. He positioned himself behind one of the boxelders, put his armload onto the ground, and covered his head. Another explosion, followed by four more, in quick succession, echoed against the high cliff ruins, then faded away. Maybe that was the last of them.

The sound of a truck engine faded into the distance. He waited for several more minutes.

He gathered the figurines and held them to his chest. These were going to his uncle, up on the mesa, whose clan had made the clay sculptures generations ago. He thought for a moment about the long, hard journey they were making, the tough journey everyone in this world was making, and the importance of circling home.

That crooked crew had an ingenious plan, he had to admit. Stealing the most valuable artifacts from local museums, small towns with lax security, then giving the antiquities new identities, new locations, new provenance, all designed to keep the collectors happy. And to garner top dollar. But it was theft, pure and simple, not just of physical property but part of his family's art and legacy and history.

Relic gathered his things and stood. He glanced at the open ground from behind the trees and brush then crossed the creek to the other side, where his pack was hidden. He knew a way out, back up Ghost Creek gorge where he and Owen had come down, back to the spring, then farther up an arroyo there, onto the plateau. From there, he could trek north into any of several canyons, depending on how much daylight he had left.

All hell was coming down on this little site, in short order, and he had no intention of being here when it did.

CHAPTER 61

They had to shout at each other to hear over the rumble of the engine, so they settled into a long stretch of silence. They'd reached an area where the canyon walls fell away, the lands opened wide, and the two-lane highway dodged hillocks and arroyos as it meandered toward civilization. They seemed to be flying much higher now that the canyon walls were not so close to their wings, an illusion Owen welcomed. He marveled at how different the world was from up here, in the thin desert air, level with the mesas, atop fingered canyons reaching out from the Colorado River, a whole new perspective on our precious planet, and on life.

They continued to follow the highway for another half-hour and began to see small clusters of buildings in the distance.

"There!" Suzy pointed ahead of them. "See the runway?"

Owen strained but could not make it out.

"Parallel to the road, in front of a row of hangars…"

"I see it!"

"OK now. Pull back on the power, just a little bit."

Owen reduced speed, the plane dipped downward, and he glanced at her.

"That's good for now. Let's get a little lower and we'll line up with the runway."

Owen's stomach clenched. He'd gotten used to the smoothness of flight, the steady run of the engine, the feel of the controls, but landing scared the hell out of him.

"I'll try, but I don't know how…"

Suzy leaned closer to him. "Trust me?"

He nodded.

"We'll line up with the runway and we'll take our time getting low to the ground. At the moment we land, we'll pull slowly back on the yoke. But I promise," she smiled, "if we don't like the look of things, we'll just go around the field."

"We can do that?"

"Sure. If we're not lined up just right, push in the throttle and we'll circle around and try it again."

"Got it." Try again if it's not just right. He liked that idea and took a breath.

They flew on for nearly ten minutes, the runway growing larger as they watched.

"You'll control the foot petals and the yoke, but I can tell you how we're doing, and you can adjust." She looked intently out her side window.

"Everything OK?"

"Yeah, I'm just looking for the wind sock."

"That thing?" Owen pointed out his window and Suzy leaned over to see.

"Yep, that's it. Looks good. You can see it's mostly just hanging there, so we know the wind is low."

Owen nodded.

"OK. Turn gently to the right."

Owen dipped the wings.

"Now pull back and turn a little to the left. Line up with the runway, straight in, best you can."

Owen rocked the wings left and levelled out. He could see the tarmac directly ahead of them, maybe three miles away.

"We're still too high, Owen, so let's make a gentle

three-sixty turn, full circle." She moved the yoke to their left and Owen found himself staring straight down at the ground as the little plane pirouetted on one wing, pushing him into his seat, spinning his inner ear like a carnival ride and it went on and on like that, houses and cars growing in size…

"Level her out."

Owen gently turned the yoke to his right until the wings were parallel with the horizon, his ear sliding back into his head, his stomach back under his belt. The runway appeared out the front window, looking awfully skinny but awfully close at the same time.

"OK, now pull the power off completely and we'll glide on in."

Shit, Suzy, don't make it sound so damned easy. He tugged the throttle out until the engine barely idled and the plane dropped closer to the ground.

"See the number 21 on the pavement?"

"Yes."

"Aim for any place just past that. Keep your eyes on the 21 'till you pass it, then focus on the end of the runway."

Owen couldn't help but glance from the number to the end of the tarmac and back again, but he began to get the feel of it. Keep your eyes on the distance and you'll set her down gently, he thought.

"Good. Good."

"When should I pull back?"

"Start now, but keep it slow and steady. Only pull back, don't push forward."

They tilted back as the Aeronca angled upwards and the front view filled with nothing but sky. He had to lean his head against the window to keep the runway in sight. Engine in the periphery, he reminded himself, end of the tarmac as the target.

"Hold that angle for a minute."

The white numbers 21 flashed out of sight below them and Owen knew he was in range for the landing. A soft breeze turned him toward the hangars and he quickly angled the wings the opposite direction and levelled out again.

The pavement rose quickly toward them and Owen pulled again on the yoke and held it there, steady, steady, small adjustments to keep her level, and the stall warning squealed and suddenly they jolted onto solid ground, the wheels squeaking, safe, finally safe on the ground, and for a flash he began to relax but they bounced upward again, too high he thought, into panic, then down, tires squeaking a second time but now they were fully landed, no longer floating in the air.

The back of the plane dipped to the ground, the rear wheel touching down, when a gust of wind spun the plane toward a row of buildings and they were suddenly off the runway.

CHAPTER 62

They crossed a median of sorts, bucking and bouncing, Owen shoving the right pedal into the floor to no avail. They spun again in the slippery grass, all the way around, then bumped onto pavement near the hangars and screeched to a stop.

He didn't remember shutting down the engine, but he must have. The propeller was no longer a blur and the quiet seemed to pound against his head.

Suzy poked a finger in one ear and wiggled it then shook her hair out of her face and glanced back at him. Her eyes seemed to have teared, but her smile made the universe sing and she reached across and grasped his hand.

"I knew you could do it."

He knew he had a goofy grin on his face but couldn't help himself. He wasn't able to speak or move or think, but his own smile must have conveyed it all because Suzy's eyes seemed to tear again and she blinked and squeezed his fingers.

"Are you guys all right?" The voice came from behind them and they shifted in their seats.

"Helluva landing." A rounded, ruddy face appeared under the wing on Suzy's side and the man opened her door. "Gotta watch those tail draggers, they'll spin out on you before you know it. You guys OK?"

"Yeah, sort of." Suzy lifted her swollen ankle out of the plane and let it hang above the ground. She slid carefully onto her other foot and hobbled out of the Aeronca.

Owen opened his door and turned gingerly on the old towel that covered his seat. His feet touched ground, the feeling foreign. He grabbed the strut and held on for balance.

"When I couldn't raise you on the radio, I figured you might be in trouble. Now I see you don't have one." The man pointed at the instrument panel.

"Right." Owen moved slowly from under the wing and to the front of the plane.

"The fabric on this old bird's shot to shit. Where the hell did you guys come from?" The man removed a cap from his head and scratched.

"Ghost Creek." Owen ran his fingers along the edge of the propeller.

"Hey, we need to call 911." Suzy leaned on the strut and hopped toward the engine. "There's a truck load of students on their way out of there and some crazy people with guns behind them."

The man's eyes widened.

"Send the sheriff there right away, please!" Owen clasped his hands together.

The man reached for his phone and walked away from them, speaking urgently into the mouthpiece.

"And tell them it's the museum thieves they've been looking for!"

The man nodded as he spoke into the phone.

"Hey, look." Suzy pointed to a rusty sign on the door of the hangar, directly in front of them. An old-style bi-plane was sketched on the surface. Above it read, "Learn to fly: fifty cents." Below it read, "Learn to land: two dollars."

Owen smiled. "Sounds about right."

She hopped toward him and reached for his hand. "Willing to give it a go?" He wondered if she meant more than just flying lessons.

"I am if you are..."

She squeezed his fingers.

"Hey," he glanced at his feet then back to her smile. "Have you ever seen a real bullet wound?"

CHAPTER 63

Relic climbed to the rim where it started to rise from the creek and sat for a moment. He put his binoculars to his eyes and searched the canyon. When he found the dirt road, he followed it from camp to a spot a couple of miles away, around the low hill to where it began to run parallel to the wide Colorado River, and studied a shiny speck that sat there.

It was the silver pickup truck Johnson drove out of camp. Two men walked around the vehicle in a circle, finding a tire flat. He followed the road farther south along the river but could not see the truck the students had taken, and the old Aeronca seemed long gone. Good for them.

He adjusted his view toward the camp and the large blue tent and the tarp canopy next to the hangar. He couldn't see anyone there, but they might be inside.

Not that they could do much, now, except hike out of there. But Angela and Everett weren't exactly the hiking type, and he thought he heard a distant wail of sirens to the south, where the dirt road met the highway.

He put the binoculars into his pack. A lonesome crow floated above the creek, planning a raid, no doubt, on the goodies in the kitchen down below.

Relic stared across the canyon, taking one last glance at the Ghost Creek Pueblo ruins. He could hear the squeals of children, the songs of women, the grunt of masons pulling stones to the top of the cliff and, when he took a deep breath, he could imagine the smell of their fires, roasted turkey, pipe tobacco, fresh corn, and it just didn't seem all that long ago.

AUTHOR'S NOTE

This work is offered in memory of my friend Norman Willow. An elected member of the Northern Arapaho Business Council for many years, Norman was a seasoned leader. He was an honest and generous man who worked hard for the people he served and when it came to defending the sovereignty of the Tribe, he had a backbone of iron. And he had the talent and timing of a professional comedian – no one could break up a room of serious people with more style, humor, and poignancy than Norman Willow. He continues to be sorely missed, but his inspiration lives on.

ACKNOWLEDGEMENTS

I want to acknowledge my parents, family, colleagues, and many accomplices. Thanks to all who understand their kinship with the planet and those who work in the service of their ideals.

Forever thanks to Dad for showing me the magic of flight and inspiring me to become a pilot. Thanks also for his kind technical assistance in making sure the flying scenes in Wings Over Ghost Creek were accurate and realistic.

Thanks to my incredible wife Gina and my wonderful family for letting me disappear for hours and days at a time while working on this story. Thanks also to Gina, Dad, Sarah, and my sister Julie (an accomplished author!) for their valued comments and contributions. I could not have written it without them.

I also want to thank my editor, Jim Dempsey, for his encouragement, careful attention to detail, and insightful suggestions. I could not have finished this without his talented help. And I thank Daniel Thiede for his incredible cover art and book design and for his invaluable help with the technical aspects of the work. Thanks to Nate for the map art!

I also want to thank my friends at Holiday Expeditions for their warm support. You won't find a finer group of people or better hosts for your canyon whitewater or biking adventures. They are real pros, in business since 1966. Visit them at www.bikeraft.com.

Finally, I thank Tex's Riverways, both the prior and the current owners, for their years of professional service and conscientious protection of Canyonlands. Grab a canoe and visit them at texsriverways.com.

EXCERPT FROM

RAPTOR CANYON

The tent became a dome of light, then began to smolder and burst into flame near the back, near the kitchen stove.

"Hey, we just cleaned the grill back there," Relic said, making Wyatt laugh.

The fire spread slowly, casting a halo of light across the camp. Security guards hollered, workers yelled their curses and questions, and everyone rushed to see what the commotion was all about.

"Is she really crazy enough to do that?" Wyatt asked.

"Yep," Relic nodded.

"Well, shee-it," Wyatt did his best imitation of Faye.

Relic smiled. "Don't let her hear you or she'll knock your block off."

"No doubt."

"Would you see what you can do to slow down that backhoe up ahead of us and anything else with a lock and key? Then work your way north, swing back toward the staircase and we can meet up there."

Wyatt nodded.

"Keep a close look out. They'll be searching as soon as the mess [kitchen tent] is under control."

"What's your next move?" Wyatt asked.

Relic jerked his thumb toward the portable toilets.

"Really?" Wyatt said.

Relic turned and faded into the dark. Wyatt heard footfalls, someone moving quickly toward him. After a moment, he recognized her shape bobbing along. She tossed something and he heard it clacking into the bed of a pickup. She nearly ran into him.

"Hey." He put his hands out toward her.

"Hey," she said, slowing, but only a bit. "Here." She tossed a stick of dynamite to him, the fuse sparkling lit.

"Shit!"

"Throw it!" she shouted as she ran past. "Now!"

Wyatt stared at the tube in his hand. The fuse sputtered and spat and shortened with every second, time compressed with the tightness of his breath, the glowing fuse moving forward immutably until something like a spinning clutch popped in his chest and muscle movement became possible again. He reached his arm back and threw it as far and as fast as he could, then he spun and ran to the side of another truck and turned back to look.

The pickup Faye had tossed something into rose into the air with a smack that washed away all other sound, then fell back to the ground with a nasty twist as pieces of sheet metal dropped from the sky.

"Holy…"

Wyatt's stick of dynamite exploded somewhere beyond another truck, lighting something on fire, sending a second sonic boom through his skull, making him jump in his tracks. He stared at the blaze as it settled into a steady burn and looked the direction Faye had run.

A third, fourth, and fifth explosion erupted in quick succession in the row of portable toilets and Wyatt knew it was Relic's work. Where was Relic's peaceful resistance now? Lord, he hoped no one was in those toilets. Then, he thought, what a mess of shit, and he giggled and smacked his hands together.

Oh, my god, was it possible to have so much fun? He never expected stopping Lord Winnieship from stealing this canyon to feel so damn good.

He stared at the fire he'd started and tried to think. He wanted to follow Faye but there was no telling what other mayhem she had in mind, and he did not want to walk into an exploding outhouse. He tried to regulate his breathing, with only a little luck.

He circled away from the path Faye had taken, giving her a wide berth, moving to the outer edge of the parked vehicles.

Wyatt turned and trotted toward a lone backhoe, maybe sixty yards away. Though the electric lights of the compound were out, the kitchen and dining room blaze cast a sallow glow on the tops of the other tents and equipment. The upper arm of the yellow backhoe was lit like a candle.

His shins scraped across brittle sage and he slowed to a walk. He'd lost his own toothpicks, so that trick [of jamming the locks] would not work with the heavy equipment. After Faye's dynamite, toothpicks seemed pretty pathetic anyway. Maybe there was a set of keys kept in the ignition that he could toss away. Or maybe he could flatten its tires or pull wires from under the dash to disable the beast. He turned to watch the bobbing of flashlights all around the burning mess tent a quarter of a mile away. The voices of men rose and fell in a rhythm that was almost musical, like an offbeat composition.

He stopped at the base of the backhoe and stared up at the top, where the boom and dipper attached. He circled the machine to the open cabin and peered inside.

"Stop and turn around." The voice was deep and familiar.

Wyatt turned and raised his hands. Even in the semi-dark, Lynch's muscled bulk identified him immediately. He held a pistol aimed at Wyatt's chest.

"You!" Lynch said. "You sonofabitch."

Wyatt saw the left hook a milli-second before it struck his jaw, wrenching his head away and toward the ground. He stumbled to the side. A blow to his stomach struck like a rocket and his chest ached, all the veins in his body shut down by a sonic boom. Slivers of light flashed through his eyes, closed tight against the assault. He sensed himself floating to the earth, his muscles turned to liquid. He was out before he hit the dirt.

EXCERPT FROM

DESERT GUARDIAN

The roar of whitewater drowned out all other sounds of life, even Ethan's own breathing. He watched with a sense of awe as Anya powered her boat to the left, deftly guiding it as she watched the rapids on their right.

Ethan followed her move, paddling to line up with the left shore, then rowing toward it.

In mere moments, a huge rock appeared on their right, the river bellowing over it like a jet engine. Water reared high above the rock, spraying whitecaps into the air, plunging into a crater of water below, swirling and rising and collapsing on itself as it went. He could feel the waves rocking his raft even several yards away. As quickly as the sound had engulfed him, it started to fade.

"Ethan!" Anya yelled across, her voice a mere reminder among the sound of throbbing rapids to look up, pay attention.

He saw her rowing toward the right shore. Quickly, he spun the raft so his back was to the same shore and began to row.

The current was much faster here than in the stretch of flat water he'd gotten used to. He could hear and sense the rapids directly in front of him. He dipped the oars and pulled mightily with mediocre results. He forced himself to row faster and harder, desperate to avoid the coming whitewater.

The sound of the first rapid he'd passed was nothing compared to the vibration and roar of the waves ahead. All he could do was keep rowing, putting his legs into it, straining his back against the oars.

Without warning, the front of his raft dipped sideways into a trough, nearly tossing him out of the boat. His upriver oar swung through thin air, angled out of the water. He leveled out for a moment, bracing himself. Then the raft buckled inward as it crashed into a wave ten feet above his head. His hands slipped from the oars and found brief purchase on the center frame. The river pounded him like a waterfall. He lost all sense of direction as the raft spun high on the cresting water, spray blasting his skin like shotgun pellets.

The raft slid sideways across the downriver slope of the high wave. He was weightless for a moment as it fell toward another trough and then, at the bottom, the raft buckled again, tossing him clear of the boat like a piece of cork.

He had time for only half a breath before the cold water sucked him under, spinning him down through the roiling currents. He struggled for a second, flailing his arms and legs, then stopped. As water pressure began to hurt his ears, he knew he was too deep to swim up, that he'd use his air too quickly if he tried to fight the current. Let the life jacket do its job, he thought, if it can. He forced himself to relax, to conserve his energy, to let the river take him where it would. To do that, he had to surrender - fully, unconditionally – to the power of the water, the flow of rain, snowmelt, and desert springs all merged into one gargantuan muscle of river tearing through bedrock itself, carving grand canyons out of solid stone. What could anyone do against that?

His arms and legs tingled painfully then went numb - from the cold or lack of oxygen he could not tell. His mind flashed to Relic's water bottle. Water, the one thing he could not live without in this harsh and beautiful desert; the one thing that would now kill him. He would never take water for granted again.

Though his eyes were closed, stars and spears of light flashed across them. He spun more slowly than before but disorientation had seized control. Was he right side up? Rising? Sinking?

His chest burned like molten magma, cooking and crackling, dying for a simple gasp of air to release the flame. His muscles moved involuntarily to expel his breath but he forced them back. He knew he had to breathe, and soon, even if it meant sucking his lungs full of water, but he rallied back against the thought, squeezing it out, willing himself to never breathe again. When his throat convulsed, the world became a void.

Sign up for book announcements and special deals at:

AWBALDWIN.COM

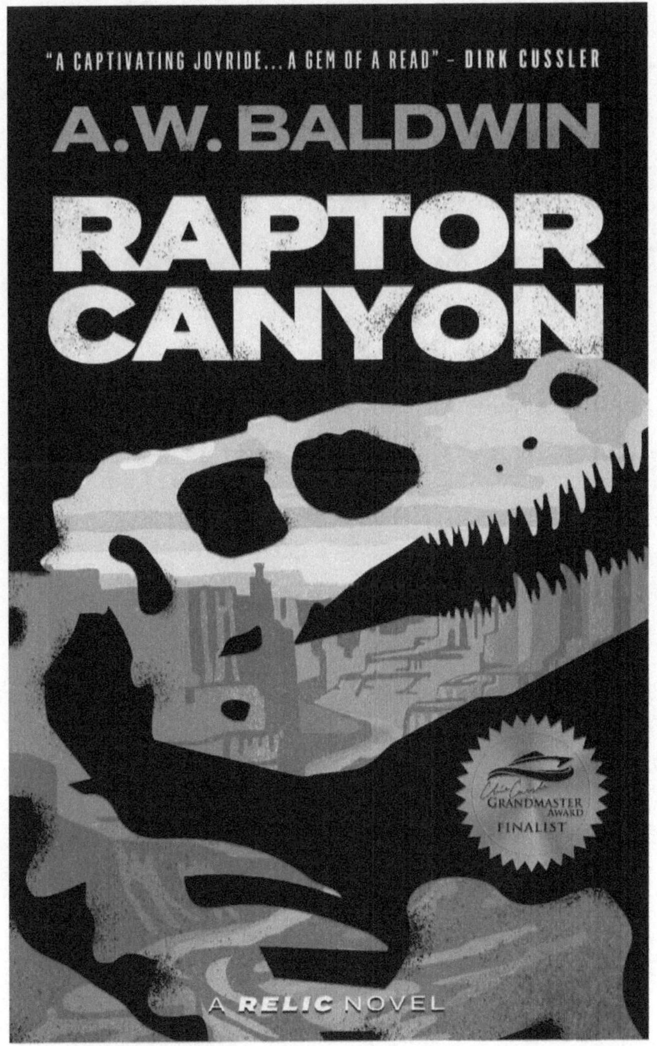
"A CAPTIVATING JOYRIDE...A GEM OF A READ" – DIRK CUSSLER
A.W. BALDWIN
RAPTOR
CANYON
GRANDMASTER
AWARD
FINALIST
A RELIC NOVEL

What if you discover you've helped your boss hide a murder and defile a pristine canyon? Can a young lawyer and moonshining hermit save rare petroglyphs and monkey-wrench a corrupt land deal in the Utah canyons?

An impromptu murder leads a hermit named Relic to an unlikely set of dinosaur petroglyphs and swindlers using the unique rock art to turn a pristine canyon into a high-end tourist trap. When attorney, Wyatt, and his boss travel to the site to approve the next phase of financing, Wyatt learns the truth about their unorthodox role in the project. A corrupt security chief runs Relic and Wyatt off of the site and the unusual pair must endure each other while fleeing though white-water rapids, remote gorges, and hidden caverns. Faye, who shares covert ties with the treasured site, catalyzes their desperate plan to fight back and to recast the fate of Raptor Canyon.

Buy now from a bookstore near you or amazon.com

Can a student, desert recluse, and whitewater crew save Aztec treasures and an ancient pueblo battlefield from looters?

Ethan's world turns upside-down when he slips off the edge of red-rock cliffs into a world of twisting canyons, ruthless looters, and midnight murders. Saved by a moonshining hermit, Ethan must join a whitewater rafting group and make his way back to civilization. But someone in the canyons is killing to protect their illegal dig for ancient treasures. Ethan must learn who he can and cannot trust, survive the harsh desert, and unravel the mysterious murders. The fight of his life begins now…

Buy now from a bookstore near you or amazon.com